Pr

TENNIS FROM THE HEART

Pursuing the Dream

"Only a holistic tennis educator and a spiritually-oriented person of the caliber of Ted Murray, could have written this book. The story of Sam is pregnant with valuable life lessons...lessons that will serve any serious tennis player well if they aspire to be of championship material."

—Dr. Desmond Oon, Author, *Conversation with a Zen Tennis Master* and *Can Eastern Wisdom Improve Your Tennis? You Bet.*

"An empowering, and refreshingly, insightful story for all tennis enthusiasts and fans, written by a seasoned professional with an infectious love and passion for the game. This inspiring story serves as a persuasive guidebook, offering simple, practical, and essential instructions for parents, coaches, and players to teach and play the game from their heart. By holistically combining effective, coaching methods with caring values, this book will surely evolve the game we all love."

—Randall Scott, tennis professional in Asia with a broad range of experiences in the tennis industry. He has devoted the last twenty years of his career building tennis academies and programs, and currently specializes in developing and coaching elite players competing on the different junior and senior tours using a refined, holistic, development approach.

"Ted Murray's heart-centered coaching and inspirational guidance has been instrumental in me realizing my dream of being an Olympic medalist and Grand Slam Champion."

—Leander Paes – 6 time Olympian and 15 time Grand Slam Doubles Champion, Singles bronze medalist at 1996 Olympics.

Ted Murray in *Tennis from the Heart* connects us almost instantly with Sam's challenges as an athlete and tennis player. He expertly takes us along on his journey of transformation through heart centered techniques. You will laugh and cry along with Sam! You will learn and grow along with Sam. You will definitely enjoy the journey! I highly recommend *Tennis from the Heart* to anyone who wants to learn the power of "playing from love!"

—Linda Le Claire, author of *The Confidence Factor* and *Yes, God Speaks to Women, Too! A Message of Health, Healing and Hope*

"Ted Murray has woven a wonderful Life and Sport Philosophy into Tennis from the Heart. This story brings Laughter, Tears of Joy and a great Awareness of our Potential to truly play Tennis from the Heart!"

—Dr. Bryce Young Doctor of Sport Psychology, Author of *The Courtside Coach: A Personal Mental Trainer for Tennis Players*

"Tennis from the Heart is a great read for anyone who plays the game of tennis at any level". Very insightful story line about how a player thinks, how important coaching can be to a player and the choices you make in life that affect the path taken in achieving your dreams. You can tell Ted is a true student of the game at all levels. This is a must read for juniors and adults who are looking for guidance, mentoring and confirmation that we all experience fears along our journey in life and in sports."

—Ken DeHart, AVAC Director of Tennis, PTR International Master Pro, USPTA Master Pro, USA High Performance Coach, Wilson Premier Advisory Staff

TENNIS FROM THE HEART

Pursuing the Dream

Dec. 2019

Dear Lowell,

I feel so blessed to be married to Donalie and be part of your unique and wonderful family. Hope you enjoy and are inspired by the book to live and play from the Heart!

Lots of love,

Ted J Murray

TED MURRAY

Published by Mason Works Press; Boulder, Colorado.

Ted Murray would love to hear from readers. Please email him at:
ted@tennisfromtheheart.com and visit www.tennisfromtheheart.com

For information, please contact Kathy Mason, Publisher, at kathy@mason-works.com, or write to Mason Works Press, 6525 Gunpark Dr.#370-426, Boulder, CO 80301.

ISBN 978-0-942097-88-7 (Paper)
ISBN 978-0-942097-89-4 (Kindle)

First Edition

Interior Design by Veronica Yager, YellowStudios
Cover design by Mason Works Press

Library of Congress Control Number: pending

Printed in United States of America

Acknowledgements

Many people have been instrumental in my life beginning with my parents, Jim and Mary Murray who made unimaginable sacrifices to provide opportunities for me.

My long and rewarding international career as a tennis professional was made possible by Peter Burwash, an amazing teacher and mentor. My first time living in India changed my life, and I must thank Vijay Amritraj and his family for creating a unique academy, the BAT program. Coaching Leander Paes as a 12-year old really showed me what a dream and determination can do, and he remains a close friend after 25 years as one of the top doubles players in the world.

The editor who inspired me to finish the book and gave much valuable advice about writing a novel is Kathy Conde. My beautiful soul mate, Kathy Mason, is the one who is most responsible for actually getting the book printed and into your hands.

Many, many more people have had an influence on my life, especially all of the students I have had the privilege to coach through the years. I would like to thank them, and dedicate this book to the next generation of children who will be inspired to play the wonderful sport of tennis with joy, freedom, and passion….. playing from the HEART!

Chapter One

Sam toed the line of the dusty, worn baseline three and one half feet to the left of the center service line. He lifted his cap (part of his serving ritual for the serve) momentarily exposing his sandy-blond hair. His mind was racing and his nerves were tight. On the second of his customary three bounces the ball hit a rough patch, bounced off and rolled toward the service line. The entire crowd of 14,932 who had been enthralled by the four-hour thirty-two-minute battle of this five set semi-final knew that Sam was nervous. Who wouldn't be when serving a second serve at match point to enter the finals at Wimbledon?

As the ball girl tossed him another ball he tried not to think of what it would be like to double fault and lose what might be his only opportunity to win the match. He was utterly exhausted and knew that he could not survive another two or possibly ten games required to win the fifth set with no tiebreaker. He had given all he had to break serve at 6-all and now serve for the match. Already he had saved two break points this game and had gotten a lucky bounce off the baseline to reach this point. He couldn't blow it now.

He forced himself to clear all thoughts of double faulting from his mind. Instead he thought back to the years he had spent at the academy where every afternoon practice had started with hitting thirty aggressive serves in the correct service box in a row. Was this pressure any greater than having all of your peers waiting for you to finish so they could start practice? He knew what it felt like to miss on ball twenty-eight and hear the groans of disbelief from the others. After the first year he became so tough that he was never the one who missed. In fact he had begun to love the challenge of hitting his most daring serves at that point.

A daring serve was certainly what was needed here. He had to end the point quickly and not get engaged in a long baseline rally. Although at five feet ten inches Sam was considered short for a modern tennis player, he had an excellent kick serve wide to the backhand. He knew this was the serve that gave his opponent trouble, but only if it kicked high and wide to his two-handed backhand, forcing him to stretch completely. If Sam slowed his wrist acceleration even a tiny bit the serve would be right in his opponent's strike zone and he would likely hit another winning return or put Sam under so much pressure that he would be on the defensive.

Sam took his time while taking long, deep belly breaths to calm himself. Deep breathing allowed him to connect to the higher power that had been a constant source of inspiration in his life. He decided to trust that power in himself and visualized his kick serve wide. He suddenly became aware of the absolute silence that had descended on the crowd. He took his customary three bounces while shaking his Volki V1 racket to relax his wrist. Taking another deep breath he further relaxed the wrist by resting the throat of the racket in the last two fingers of his left hand. With nothing but the positive image of his ideal serve in his mind he started his windup. He allowed his body to coil to impart maximum racket-head speed, throwing the racket tip up at the ball as he had trained it so often in the hundreds of thousands of practice serves he had hit throughout his life. With an explosive jump into the air accompanied by a mighty exhalation of air, Sam put everything he had into the serve.

At impact Sam knew it was a great serve. His opponent was as surprised as the crowd that Sam had the guts to hit a daring serve that landed three inches from the sideline and kicked viciously. The opponent, who had moved in two steps anticipating a nervous, short delivery, was now out of position and forced to lunge back and wide, beyond the doubles line, to reach the ball. With an amazing effort completely extending his six foot four inch frame he got his racket on the ball but could only manage to weakly push it over the net. As the ball floated tantalizingly close to the net Sam took no chances. He was moving forward as soon as he hit the serve.

The weak return cleared the net by only six feet and sat up meekly for Sam. The easiest shots in the game are often the ones that are blown on key points and turn out to be the momentum changers in a match. Sam would not allow any of those thoughts to enter his mind. He moved in confidently, allowed the ball to sit up into his shoulder level comfort zone, took his racket back with the face closed and accelerated the racket head through the ball with confidence. He took no chances, aiming three feet inside the sideline, and drove the ball crosscourt, well out of reach of his desperately scrambling opponent. Sam was in the finals at Wimbledon!

What a feeling, as he knelt down and lifted his head in thanks. Relief, joy, exhaustion, and clarity flowed through him all at the same time, making his entire body tingle. The green grass was soft under his knees. He gave up the struggle to hold back tears of joy, realizing he had taken a huge step toward the dream he had so often visualized as a child but had long ago given up hope of ever attaining. Now he would have a day and a half to prepare himself for taking that final leap toward actually achieving that dream. For a few moments, time seemed to stand still as his emotions engulfed him. Then reality set in as his mind began to shift from this match to his preparation for the final. Time was not his yet. After flinging his wristbands, headband, and shirt into the crowd, he prepared to be interviewed by Jim Courier, a player he had always admired as a truly exceptional human being who actually achieved beyond his talent level to win four grand slams.

Jim's first question was predictable, "How does it feel to be in the Wimbledon final when in your previous ten years on the tour you never made it past the round of sixteen in any Grand Slam event?"

Sam struggled to put into words the emotions that were going through his mind and body. All he could say was he felt like he was in the middle of the universe and was feeling all kinds of emotions simultaneously. He expressed his incredible gratitude for all of those who had helped him on the long and uncertain path that had led him to this point.

Jim's next questions was, "How did you have the guts to hit such a bold second serve on match point?"

"It was simply a matter of trusting," Sam said. "I knew I was capable of such a serve under the greatest pressure of my life. I simply trusted in my own ability and in the higher power that guides my heart to make it successful."

The rest of the interview was simply a haze for Sam. Leaving center court was no easy task. Back when he was struggling to find his game and was seldom playing in front of more than fifty people in the stands, he had promised never to refuse an autograph for any kid. He always remembered how he had felt when he was a shy, skinny nine year old and went to the US Open for the first time. His favorite player at the time had walked right past him without stopping to sign or even acknowledge Sam's presence as he walked briskly from the practice court to the players' lounge. That day, Sam vowed never to root for that player again. A few years later he was thrilled when his new idol, Roger Federer, not only gave him an autograph but actually asked his name and what his dream was.

"My dream is to win Wimbledon," Sam had answered.

"That's a worthy dream," Roger said. "Keep working hard and have faith that even the most impossible sounding dream can become a reality. It certainly has for me!"

Sam became a Roger Federer fan for life. His desire to work hard to achieve that seemingly unreachable dream that is shared by hundreds of thousands of other kids skyrocketed. He never missed a chance to follow Roger's success. Now it was possible that his name could be engraved on the most hallowed trophy in tennis alongside Roger's remarkable seven inscriptions. Now, that unlikely dream was only one match away from becoming a reality. Yet he still spent the next forty-five minutes engagingly signing autographs, knowing that this act might indeed fuel a young kid's passion to become the champion in another ten or twelve years.

As he made his way to the locker room, it seemed like his exhaustion had been rejuvenated by the eager adulation of all of his newly discovered young fans. The press room was overflowing with reporters wanting to make the most of this incredible story of a perennial journeyman pro making such a huge breakthrough in this most hallowed stage in all of sports. Although he tried to answer each question completely and accurately, all he could really express was the joy and gratefulness he felt at that moment to have the opportunity to fulfill his ultimate dream. Sam answered from his heart and allowed his honest feelings to simply flow out. He was also becoming aware of the passing of time and the disruption of his normal recovery routine after a match. Even though this had been a tremendous accomplishment, he still had to keep his mind focused on the ultimate achievement, performing to his full potential in the final.

When he finally reached the locker room and got into the shower, all energy drained out of his body, and he could barely stand. His knees had difficulty supporting his one hundred sixty-five pounds of toned muscle as wave after wave of emotion passed through him again. For the first time, he grasped the enormity of his accomplishment and it nearly brought him to his knees. In fact he did drop to his knees to offer a most sincere and heartfelt prayer and humbly gave thanks for being given the strength to make this achievement a reality. He promised to dedicate this victory and all future success to living his life in a way that would inspire millions of other children to follow their passion and never give up on their dreams, no matter how unrealistic they might seem.

When he finally made it to the massage table he was completely spent. It was well past midnight, but Sam couldn't change the routine that had worked so well for him. He knew how essential massage was to his rapid recovery. His favorite therapist, Maria, had been waiting for him, despite having had a long and challenging day. Just the smell of the essential oil and the soothing music transported Sam into a state of complete relaxation. Maria's energy was still very strong, and as Sam felt her compassionate and knowing hands search out and soothe every ache and pain, he felt her energy helping him replenish his. He had always loved the energy exchange that takes place in a good massage. It was often more important than the physical relief a massage provided aching muscles. He always sought out the therapist who seemed to be connected to an inexhaustible supply of energy. In this way the connection through the hands became almost like a sacred union that increased the energy of both the masseuse and the one receiving the massage.

After another shower, and giving Maria a deep and grateful hug along with a five hundred dollar tip, Sam suddenly realized he was famished. In all the excitement he had neglected one of the cardinal rules of athletic recovery, the need to eat a balance of quality protein along with carbohydrates within thirty minutes of any strenuous workout. Fortunately, he had kept a bottle of his now famous homemade energy drink at his side. He had finished two liters of the secret mix of coconut water, jaggary (a natural sugar from India), and a few other powerful ingredients. Now he needed something solid that wouldn't keep him awake at night. He was glad he had decided to become a vegetarian twelve years ago, after experimenting with any number of diets designed to help him improve his overall health and athletic performance. This had enabled him to eat even at crazy hours of the night after tough matches without worrying about the slow digestion process affecting his all-important sleep.

He was afraid the players' lounge would be completely shut down and nothing would be available. He had no desire to wait until taking the thirty-minute ride to the hotel and trying to get something at the restaurant that would be jammed with newly found fans who would want to share the victory with him. Right now he just wanted some peace and nutrition to help him recover and sleep well. As he opened the door to the players' lounge he was delighted to see Sven, one of the younger attendants there, but one who had always treated Sam with the same respect shown Federer and the other champions. This was unusual in the normal world of treating the players according to their ranking and reputation, and treating the non-stars almost as if they didn't even exist. Perhaps it was because Sven had also become a vegetarian and took a special interest in the nutritional well being of one of the few fully committed vegetarians on the tour. Although many of the players over the years had moved toward a meat-free diet most were still under the impression that they could never get enough protein without at least eating chicken and fish. Sam was proving that wasn't necessary, as his energy that day against a player seven years his junior had proven.

Sam gratefully accepted Sven's offering of his favorite grilled vegetable sandwich on special gluten-free toast. Learning of his allergy to gluten and several other foods had been an important breakthrough for Sam, and he was glad that all tournaments were taking a greater interest in providing nutritious alternatives to players who had discovered how much food allergies of all kinds could affect their health. Sam would have loved nothing more than to have had French fries along with his sandwich, but he had decided to drastically limit his intake of fries after learning how damaging and filled with fat they can be. Instead he took an extra scoop of cottage cheese, one of his favorite sources of protein. He also ate a handful of almonds and walnuts, another of his favorite protein sources. He especially liked nuts as a snack that he would eat at regular intervals throughout the day. He topped his meal off with a special protein shake made with his favorite whey protein, banana and peanut butter. He had loved that combination since his childhood when he had to prepare his own lunches and became an expert at all combinations that could make peanut butter interesting and assist it in gliding down the throat instead of sticking there in a lump. In spite of this creativity with peanut butter concoctions the combination of banana with peanut butter had always been his all-time favorite. This shake always served not only as a great energy booster but also as dessert. It never failed to satisfy his sweet tooth.

In the early days of his career Sam had always carried an extra fifteen pounds of weight around his stomach, a testimony to his uncontrolled craving for sweets. It was only after making the choice to limit his intake of sweets that he had maximized both his speed and stamina on the court. He was happy that the wonderful combination in the shake could so miraculously replenish the needs of his body while also satisfying his tongue's craving for instant gratification. Even though he knew it was late and fatigue was closing in on him, he still took his time to savor every bite and every gulp of this meal that had been so lovingly prepared by Sven.

Sam reflected on how important each and every one of the volunteers was at a tournament and how much their support had meant to his success. He felt like each of them was secretly rooting for him. Perhaps that was a result of the conscious effort he always made to thank them and make them feel seen and appreciated, no matter how young or how insignificant it seemed their allotted task was. Sam knew that energetically people mirror the energy you put out to them. He realized that if he wanted love and respect from others he had to first give it to them. After years of following that philosophy on tour Sam had created a reputation as one of the truly nice guys on the circuit. Other players could never seem to figure out why Sam always got little special favors like being the first one dropped off at the hotel, getting practice courts even when they were already all booked, or getting upgraded to business class on flights even though he couldn't afford to travel there like the top fifty players.

Tonight he didn't have to worry about who was dropped off at the hotel first. He was the only player on the grounds when he finally made his way to the hotel. Sam wanted nothing more than to simply crash out on the hard yet comfortable mattress of his hotel room and drop off immediately to sleep. But no matter how tired he was it wasn't meant to be. Perhaps it was the emotion of the day or maybe just the peanut butter and banana, but as soon as his head hit the pillow (a special thin and fluffy one that he carried with him everywhere in order to avoid stiff necks caused by the typically fat, hard hotel pillows) he began to drift back into his childhood memories. He might have been dreaming, yet he knew he was not completely asleep. It was a state of consciousness between sleep and dreaming where often the most profound ideas reside, where it's possible to access the unconscious mind that has a complete memory of all events of your life.

Chapter Two

Sam thought back to the first day that he was introduced to tennis at age three. His father thought he was a little too feminine in his attachment to nature and his penchant for daydreaming and playing with imaginary beings. Sam's father wanted him to become an athlete and saw tennis as a sport that offered the greatest benefits, such as money, fame, travel, and access to high-level people. So Sam was sent to take private lessons from Dimitri , his first coach. Dimitri had played on the ATP circuit for six years, never breaking into the top two hundred. He only covered his travel expenses through the help of a couple local sponsors. He had to supplement that income with the occasional lesson in order to make ends meet.

Dimitri was obviously not really interested in working with a three year old kid whose father was pushing him to play, but he needed the money. His philosophy was that every player who came to him should become a champion, so he wanted to start Sam off with perfect form from the very beginning. All Sam remembered is how long and boring each class was. He was placed ten feet behind what seemed like a huge net and encouraged to take his racket back, turn sideways and swing up and through the ball when Dimitri tossed it gently to him. Hitting the strings was purely a matter of luck and the quality of Dimitri's toss. Sam never really knew what the purpose of hitting these balls was or what any of the lines meant. All he knew was that Dimitri was a bearded, giant of a taskmaster who would praise him when he happened to connect with the ball that somehow made it over the net and would yell at him to watch the ball harder on the far more frequent times when his swing failed to make contact with the ball.

At almost every lesson Sam would leave the court early, crying out of boredom and frustration, feeling like he'd been in a big cage with a drill sergeant who did nothing but yell at him. How could anyone like this kind of game, Sam thought? He would much rather be out running around in nature, swimming in the stream, running with his dog, or even just sitting in his room. Anything seemed better than the forced torture of being on a tennis court.

For the next couple years Sam refused any attempts his father made to get him interested in tennis or any other sport. There was only one thing resembling sports that he liked to do. He had a yellow, soft smiley ball that he loved to throw against the wall in a hallway in the house. He loved seeing how hard he could throw it and watch the angle at which it came off. He could throw for an hour at a time, trying to vary each throw and challenge himself to still catch it on one bounce, no matter how crazy an angle he threw it. He would become so engrossed in this game with himself that his mother would have to physically pull him away from the wall when it was time to eat or do his homework.

When his parents saw that Sam loved to be engaged in solitary pursuits like this they decided that he needed to be involved in more groups, and insisted that he try other sports. For a while he regularly attended karate classes. He loved jumping and kicking and making up his own signature moves that drove his Korean instructor crazy. But once they started to make it a competition in which you were actually fighting against an opponent he began to find excuses not to attend class. He was always either injured or sick. He couldn't admit to his father, a former Army sergeant, that he couldn't stand anything resembling fighting. At least the moves he learned there helped him defend himself when the class bullies would call him a sissy, but he couldn't stand the thought of hurting another person deliberately.

He didn't hang out with other boys his age at the park and play all sorts of competitive games. Instead he preferred the company of his Aunt Harriet. Aunt Harriet was herself quite a loner, and everyone called her eccentric, if not downright crazy. Her house was filled with all types of religious and spiritual photos and paintings. She had travelled to many parts of the world on what she termed her "spiritual quest." She seemed to know everything there was to know about each and every religious and spiritual tradition in the world. Yet, unlike the priest at the local church Sam was expected to attend with his family, Harriet never claimed that any one God was the true God and all others were false. She never used fear to force people to act in a certain way as the priest did, but instead always talked about a loving and merciful Creator.

In fact, the God that she called by many different names could not have been more different from the God that was proclaimed by the local church. Sam could never see how anyone could be attracted to a God who only thought about punishing rule breakers and who seemed intent on vengeance and strict following of his commandments. He could not believe that this was the same God that Jesus talked about as a God of compassion, mercy, and love. How could the same God be so different? How could Jesus' teachings be so different than those the priests of his church were delivering every Sunday?

When Aunt Harriet talked about Jesus she told wonderful stories about how gentle and forgiving he was and how especially fond he was of children and helpless animals. She would compare him to many other spiritual teachers who have made their mark on the world. She always stressed how love was the common teaching of all such masters and that their trust in God and the loving nature of the universe was what was needed to live purposeful and spiritual lives. The stories could be from China, Tibet, Mexico, or any other country and culture. She wove them together in a way that made all traditions seem to be diverse paths created to attract people who were at different stages of their spiritual growth. She was always talking about the spiritual path, and how it was different for each and every person.

She even claimed that the path was not limited to this lifetime. Instead, she proposed that each individual was actually an eternal spirit soul who is allowed to come back birth after birth in order to learn the lessons they required to ultimately become purified and become reunited with God. When she talked like this, the neighbors really thought she was crazy. Yet, according to her, more than half of the earth's population accepts this concept of reincarnation as a matter of fact. To Sam it sure seemed to make God seem a lot more merciful, providing a chance to learn from mistakes and grow rather than having one short lifetime to determine whether you went to heaven or hell. It seemed to Sam like this would be like having only one test during your entire time at school and your results from that test determining your life's path. The difference between the glories of heaven and the fires of hell seemed way too extreme to be decided on one test, whereby someone who scored eighty percent would be rewarded with heaven while the person who got a seventy-nine percent was eternally damned to hell.

Sam didn't spend much time pondering such questions, but he loved to listen to Aunt Harriet's stories. She always made the characters come alive in talking about heroes and demons and epic battles and solitary saints. She described places of incredible beauty and isolated wonders. Sometimes Sam and Aunt Harriet would act out dramas while other times Sam would be encouraged to create movies in his mind about the stories she was telling. He got so good at visualizing things in his mind that he could see in vivid color and almost smell and feel the stories as they were being told. He became so engrossed with these stories in his mind that his teachers used to complain that he was daydreaming too much in class and not paying enough attention to their lectures. Sam's father used to yell at him when he heard reports like this from his teachers, while his mother tried to insist that it was a natural part of growing up. But Aunt Harriet came up with a plan. She knew that he needed to become more active and decided that this was a perfect time for seven-year old Sam to return to tennis.

Aunt Harriet had been a tennis enthusiast in her day. She had taken her racket on all her travels and had met a wide variety of incredible people through the sport. She used to tell Sam about the interesting people she had met and the amazing courts she had played on. She told Sam how tennis was the best sport for finding your own purpose in life and growing on your path. She explained how it forces you to take risks and go for shots while taking full responsibility for your mistakes. Like life, the tennis match presents many opportunities to make choices that determine the ultimate outcome. Being too hesitant and afraid to take risks will prevent you from beating good players just as it prevents a person from accomplishing significant things in life. But reckless risk taking without a plan and a strategy to back it up is just as foolish. A tennis match allows many opportunities to learn about yourself and the opponent while trying to make the necessary adjustments to put the odds in your favor of winning. According to Aunt Harriet, even winning or losing is not the most important aspect of the match. It is the growth process you go through during the match and the training for competition that is truly significant. One of her favorite sayings was, "It's not the destination but the journey that is most important."

As much as Sam hated the idea of trying tennis again, since it was Aunt Harriet's idea he decided to give it another try. He was enrolled in a beginner class at the YMCA. There were fourteen other kids in the class on two courts. The coach was Roland. He was short, slightly overweight and had played college tennis and taught a couple summers at local tennis camps. He was definitely more in tune with the kids than Dimitri, but he was just as obsessed with insisting on perfect form. He would have the kids line up single file and let them hit two balls at a time. He would try to toss the balls right to them and then comment about how they stood or swung the racket after each hit. Of course, Sam got totally bored, as he couldn't keep all those things in mind and still hit the ball, especially if he had to wait in line for another twenty-six balls before he got a chance to hit his next two. He was always getting in trouble for hitting balls against the fence while standing in line or trying to serve into the fence, mimicking players like Sampras and McEnroe he had seen on the videos of old matches that Aunt Harriet had shown him.

As punishment for this disruptive behavior Roland made Sam go to the other side of the net and pick up the balls while the other kids hit. Sam didn't see this as punishment at all. He saw it as liberation. He was free to run around the court and chase all types of balls with even more variety than he could create against his wall. He used to make games for himself, seeing how many he could catch on one bounce without a miss. Next he started to throw each ball he caught to his buddy Eric on the other side of the net who would return the balls to Roland's ball basket. They never let on how much they enjoyed this game. Roland seemed content since his problem of picking up all the balls was solved. He was proud of himself for coming up with such a creative solution to Sam's troublemaking. But after a couple months Sam was still struggling to hit the ball solidly. No matter how much he loved the freedom to run around and catch and throw balls, he never seemed to be able to hit it right. When he dutifully did everything exactly as Roland insisted he seldom hit the ball solidly. When he ignored the instruction and hit in a way that seemed most natural to him he was amazed at how well he could hit the ball. He loved the sound of the ball smacking squarely in the middle of the strings. Yet invariably, no matter how good the shot felt to Sam, Roland would yell at him for some part of his swing or stance being less than perfect. Sam became more and more frustrated. He couldn't understand why doing it perfectly according to Roland never led to a satisfying result, yet when he knew he had hit a great shot it was seldom acknowledged.

Sam also couldn't understand why they always stood in the same spot to hit the ball when he recognized that during a match players are constantly moving to a different position for every shot. Why did they have to stand still to try to hit the perfect shot when the game required constant movement and adjustments? It was obvious during the last five minutes of each class when Roland would have them play king or queen of the court. The players who were Roland's favorites and hit with perfect form could seldom even contact the balls coming from the opponent's shot, since they weren't moving and were instead expecting the ball to come to them. Sam and a couple others whose form was always criticized seemed to be able to return most of the balls no matter how far they had to run for them. Sam used to actually chide the perfectionists saying, "What happened to your perfect form on that shot?" or "Guess it helps if you can move to the ball?" The last five minutes and his ball collecting time is what made the class tolerable to Sam, but he still planned to quit out of pure frustration.

Aunt Harriet had to resort to bribing Sam to continue attending classes. She would promise him a special story after every class. Pretty soon Sam started to simply go through the motions during class with his mind focused on the adventure he would invariably encounter at Aunt Harriet's house afterward. He had finally decided that he would only take classes for one more week when a miracle happened. Roland hired a young new coach straight out of college to help him with the beginner kids while he focused on the advanced ones. The first time Sam met coach Jay, he knew there was something different about him. Jay was gangly and wore his hat backward. He thought like a kid, and his goal was to make the game fun for everyone in the class. Everything was a game for Jay. For the warm-up, instead of going through a dull and monotonous routine of static stretching and slow movements like high leg lifts, Jay would create a game. One day it might be dribble tag, in which all players bounced the ball down with their racket inside the service boxes. The player who was it would try to tag each of the other players in the shortest time possible. It was a great way to develop hand-eye coordination, forearm strength, agility, and broad vision.

Sam's favorite warm-up game was the throwing team game, Clean Your Room. Jay would divide the class into equal teams on opposite sides of the net. Each player would start with a ball and could stand anywhere on their side of the court. At the word *go* everyone would throw their ball across the net to the other side. The players then would catch or chase the balls thrown by the opposing team and throw it back across the net again. This would continue until at any instant in time all the balls were on the same side of the net, and the other team would be the winner. Of course, Sam was the star at this game due to his constant practice against the wall. He had the best throwing arm and the best judgment of balls coming at him, so he could usually catch balls on the fly or on the first bounce instead of having to run to the back fence to retrieve them. He also became a master of strategy, so he would position his team in the most effective manner to almost always win the game. All the kids got a great workout without even thinking about how much they were running as they were so engrossed in the game. It automatically helped develop their serve by practicing the throwing motion as well as their tracking skills that are so important in positioning to hit a good shot.

Jay's court opened up a whole new world for Sam. Instead of obsessing on every detail of form like Roland, Jay encouraged the kids to experiment and find what feels right for them. He never scolded them for making a mistake but rather gave them very simple corrections that would automatically correct the mistake. For example, if the ball went long they learned to simply close the racket angle a bit more using the non-racket hand. If it went in the net they would simply have to open the angle or aim higher over the net. When a shot went wide one way or another Jay showed them how it was simply a matter of the timing of their contact point. If contact was way in front the ball would automatically go cross-court, so the correction was just to wait a little longer. And naturally, if the ball went out down the line the correction was to hit a little earlier or further in front. This made the game simple for Sam because it actually worked. It allowed him the freedom to use his own natural swing while acting as his own coach and correcting his mistakes simply by adjusting after seeing the result. Jay seldom yelled at him unless he made the same mistake two or three times in a row. Even then he would most often just say, "Sam, was that an intelligent correction?" Or if Sam hit two or three balls in a row in the net, Jay might encourage him to hit the next ball into the back fence. He always said that overcorrecting a previous mistake was better than making the same mistake twice in a row.

Suddenly Sam was in love with tennis. He felt like he was learning something new every day. He loved experimenting and trying new shots. He loved the fact that long lines and static hitting were a thing of the past. Jay always made them move to hit the ball, and Sam loved the challenge of running all over the court to reach the balls. Sam learned how to be smart and get the ball back high over the net when he was pulled way off the court, and to attack the ball hard and low when he got a short ball that bounced up above net level. Even at such a young age he was learning the understanding of offense and defense that would serve him so well tactically throughout his career. He learned how to improvise strategies with all the different types of games that Jay came up with to challenge them. The cooperative competition type games were some of Sam's favorites, as he loved the idea of cooperating with a teammate to compete against other teams. He also loved the limitation games that Jay made up, especially since he was often the one being given handicaps to prevent him from winning all the time against the other players. His special favorites were the team competition games that always ended one of Jay's practices on a high note for all players. It made them all eager to practice the homework that Jay assigned after each class. They were also challenged to come up with at least one thing they had learned that day, thus ensuring that they were progressing in their understanding of the game every practice.

Now Sam couldn't get enough of tennis. He begged his father to let him play tennis every day. But his father insisted that he continue to go to soccer practice at least three times a week. His father realized that soccer would make him a quicker and faster athlete with better endurance. He also wanted Sam to have the experience of a true team sport to learn to cooperate with others while playing your own role for the benefit of the team. Although Sam liked soccer and was getting good at it he thrived on the challenge of the individual competition of tennis. His father helped Sam find another place in the house with more wall space so that Sam could now hit the smiley ball against the wall instead of just throwing it. Thus, even the days he didn't go to tennis practice he would hit for hours against the wall.

This extra wall practice became even more important when Jay announced that Sam and several of his mates were ready to enter their first tournament.

The first tournament was just a local ten-and-under event that didn't even count for a ranking, so none of the experienced players were there. It was primarily for beginners, and they had volunteers to help the players keep score and switch ends of the court at proper times. Sam was so nervous the night before the event that he hardly slept at all. He tried to use the visualization skills he had developed through Aunt Harriet's stories, but he couldn't even see a tennis court in his mind. He had trouble eating anything for breakfast and made sure he arrived at the tournament site at least one hour before the match was scheduled to start. He didn't realize that the scheduled match time was only an estimate, so by the time his match was called it was over two hours later, and Sam was famished. He hadn't been able to hit a ball to warm up since all courts were occupied. The five minutes allotted to warming up with the partner didn't even give him a chance to get a feel for the ball, and his legs felt like lead after sitting around for nearly three hours.

His opponent was already ten years old and was big for his age. Sam was intimidated when the kid shook his hand with a firm grip, staring down at Sam with a look of confidence, as if saying "You don't have a chance against me, punk." That is how Sam felt too. He had no confidence, and began to ask himself why he ever signed up for the tournament. His nerves were so tight that he couldn't swing the racket freely. His serve that had become quite confident suddenly deserted him. His wrist seemed to lock up on him and the free flowing throwing motion he usually felt so comfortable with was gone. The only thing that seemed in his favor was winning the toss, so he naturally assumed he had to serve. What a mistake! He double-faulted the first three points and weakly tapped in a second serve on the fourth point that was promptly dispatched by his opponent for a winner. It didn't get any better on the opponent's serve. And within twenty-five minutes Sam found himself shaking hands again, this time on the wrong end of an 8-0 score.

He was humiliated. He came off the court with his head nearly touching his knees. When his buddies asked him the score he merely shook his head in disgust. He tossed his racket to the ground and vowed at that moment to never pick it up again. Fortunately, Jay had come to the tournament to watch. Sam turned his eyes away as Jay approached him. He was prepared to tell him how horribly he played, how humiliated he was and how he never wanted to play another tournament as long as he lived. What he wasn't prepared for was Jay's first question, "What are the things you did well out there?"

Although it caught Sam by surprise he didn't hesitate an instant before saying, "Nothing. How could I have done anything well and get skunked like that?"

"Let's think about it a little deeper," Jay said. "Did you show up for the match on time?"

"Well, yes, of course I was here, even early, although I had to wait." Sam bounced his racket off his shoe.

"Just showing up is half of the formula for success," Jay said. "So you were fifty percent successful just by not being afraid to show up."

Sam gave Jay a wry smile, but he was listening.

Next question, "Did your serve improve as the match went on?" Jay gave him a steady look.

"Well, of course," Sam retorted, "it certainly couldn't have gotten any worse."

"That means you learned from your mistakes and made some corrections, right?"

"Well sure, I mean, at least I started getting them in the box finally."

"See?" said Jay, "you are already becoming your own coach."

The sun broke from behind a cloud and the heat was intense.

"Last question," Jay said. "Did you go for every ball and give your best effort on every point or did you give up?"

"Well, no, I didn't give up even though I was getting killed by the guy. I still ran after every ball, even to the end."

"Then, that means you had a successful match. If you gave your best effort on every ball throughout the match, then you played a successful match."

Sam had never heard such a thing.

"Now, the fact that you lost means you have a great opportunity to learn," Jay went on. "What did you learn that can help you improve your showing in the next tournament?"

Sam didn't have the heart to tell his coach that he had decided there would never be another tournament for him. Instead he simply reeled off a long list of things he would have to improve based on what he had learned from the match.

Jay simply listened and made notes. Then he said, "That's excellent. A very perceptive list. This means you have learned a lot from this loss. I'll add a couple more things, especially regarding warm-up and preparation for match play. This list will form the basis of our training for the next two months as we get ready for the next tournament coming up. I promise that you will be much better prepared for that tournament than you were for this one."

With that simple yet profound exchange with Jay, Sam's disgust with his performance turned into excitement about the many things he could do to improve his preparation for the next tournament. When he arrived home his father asked him if he won. His reply was, "No, I didn't win, but I sure learned a lot. I'm going to go hit balls against the wall to gain more confidence in my forehand and get ready for the next one."

"What was the score?" his dad asked. "Was it close?"

Sam called out as he headed to his wall, "It doesn't matter, Dad. What matters is that I'm going to do better in the next one." With that, he spent the next hour and a half hitting against the wall with more focus than ever before in his life. He was now a tournament player!

During the next two months of practice, Jay not only worked on all the things on Sam's list, but he had them practice many habits related to tournament play. He taught them how to warm up effectively for a match even if there were no courts or no wall available.. Sam promised to use his home wall to warm up for ten to fifteen minutes before even leaving for the tournament site. Jay talked to them about the importance of eating at least two hours before match time, mostly carbohydrates that can be rapidly digested for energy. He stressed the importance of keeping a water bottle filled with the most natural sports drink available and drinking at every changeover, even if thirst had not set in yet. They learned to pack their bag of gear the night before the event, making sure to pack an extra shirt, extra wristbands, at least two rackets, a towel and a hat. Also in the bag were easy-to-carry carbohydrate snacks that could be eaten while waiting for the match to be called or even during the changeovers between games. Bananas were great any time, while natural granola bars and other similar snacks were also beneficial.

Jay even had them practice shaking hands. He said that matches are won and lost in the initial meeting of players, as the confident player will show it by the strength of his handshake and looking the other player in the eye. The less confident player will seldom have a firm grip and will often look down and away during the meeting. To prove his point, Jay took the boys to a tournament for older and more experienced players. Without knowing any rankings or seedings Jay predicted the winner of the matches just based on the handshake before the match. When nine out of ten predictions were correct the boys were convinced that they needed to work on their handshake skills.

Once Sam asked Jay how he knew so much about all these seemingly small details about both playing and coaching when he had limited experience as a coach. Jay replied that he had learned from an excellent coach when he was growing up. This coach had taken him under his wing and had given him the knowledge and the confidence to become a number one college player at a solid NCAA Division 1 school. After finishing his successful college career and realizing that he couldn't make it to the pros Jay sought out his old coach to thank him for his help in reaching that goal and seek his advice on what he should do now. He had worked hard to earn his degree in business and had received a couple good offers from established firms.

His coach simply asked him, "What's your passion in life, business or tennis?"

That was an easy one for Jay. "Of course, it's tennis."

"Well, then, that was easy, wasn't it? You can never settle for a desk job if your passion is tennis. But if you become a tennis coach with passion you will become so successful that you will need your business degree to handle your wealth and grow your tennis enterprise."

"Wow," Jay said. "I've been agonizing for a month now on what direction I should take and you have made it so clear in one minute. How can I ever thank you for what you've done for me?"

"Promise me that you will share what you have learned from me with all your students, and share your passion for life and for tennis with them," his coach said as he stroked his well-trimmed beard. "That's the best gift you can ever give to them and to me. Then I will live on in you and in all your students."

So Jay told Sam, "I'm simply passing on to you what he taught. It worked for me, and I can see that it is working for you. I think you might even have what it takes to be a professional player one day, perhaps even a Wimbledon Champion."

Sam had never dared to even consider he could be a professional until that moment. Sure he had dreamed about playing at Wimbledon, but he thought it was just another of his youthful fantasies. Now here was a coach he respected and was growing to love saying that he had a chance. His entire perspective on tennis changed at that moment, and from then on he started to see himself as a potential Wimbledon champion.

Chapter Three

While Sam lay on the bed of his London hotel room with these thoughts of his childhood exploding through his mind he recalled Jay and how essential he had been in developing his passion for the game. If Jay hadn't shown up at a critical time in his life Sam would have given up the game before he even gave it a chance. Of all the coaches who had helped mold his game, he realized that Jay had been the most important. Sam got out his cell phone and sent off an urgent SMS to Jay. "Dear Coach. Never could have gotten where I am today without ur inspiration and guidance. Have tickets for u & ur son for finals. Happy to pay ur airfare too. Please book flights asap and get here in time. Will need ur energy to help me realize the dream u helped instill in me many years ago. Love u, Coach. Sam"

After that first tournament when he was still just a kid, all the preparation had paid off in the second tournament for Sam. He felt much more prepared and confident. He drew a pretty easy first round opponent who couldn't match his gaze during the handshake. He won confidently 8-2. The second round was a different story. He was matched against a much larger and experienced opponent. It was a windy day with leaves blowing constantly across the court. But instead of being nervous about facing a tough opponent in difficult conditions he welcomed it as a challenge. The butterflies he felt in his stomach were those of excited anticipation rather than nervous dread. He played his heart out on every point and had the guy really nervous before finally losing 8-5 to the opponent who went on to win the tournament. Sam now realized that he had the potential to win this level of tournament if he continued to improve as rapidly as he had the past two months.

The next two years sped by in a blur of tournaments. Sam established himself as one of the top twelve-and-under players in the state at the age of ten. He was even winning some of the state level tournaments. As he started to win more his father got more and more excited. He started going to all Sam's matches and became really intense in his cheering. After matches, instead of allowing Sam to do a self-assessment like Jay did, his father would launch into a critique about every aspect of the game, without even letting Sam process the match in his mind yet. His father even started coaching him when Jay wasn't at the events. Although they spent a lot of time driving together to tournaments, Sam felt like they were drifting further and further apart. Sam knew that his dad meant well, but he knew he didn't have sufficient knowledge or experience to be a coach. Besides he had never played the game, so how could he possibly understand the pressures that were building inside Sam as he competed at higher and higher levels.

The pressure to win that Sam felt coming from his father began to change Sam's game. He was no longer the relaxed competitor he was before. He no longer used his creativity or took risks with bold shots. Instead he started to play to avoid errors, probably to avoid his father's sharp exhalation of disgust every time he made an error and then the scathing critique of almost every single error at the end of the match. He became so tense when playing that he would bounce his racket on the court when he made a mistake and several times actually broke rackets out of anger. Worse yet, in an attempt to protect his ranking Sam started to make bad line calls and find ways to bend the rules to win. He would try to intimidate opponents in various ways, forcing them to give him the benefit of the doubt on close calls while he would do the opposite.

It all came to a head in the finals of the state championships. Playing against his nemesis, on the first point of the match when his serve was called out Sam asked "Are you sure?" even though it was over a foot out. He continued to question every ball his opponent called out, no matter how far out. It was a clay court, so Sam constantly went to the other side to find the mark, pointing to one that was in even though he knew it was the wrong mark. When the score was 4 – 2, he called it as 4-all. A shouting match ensued, nothing unusual for Sam. Any ball that was even close to the line Sam immediately called "out" and then pointed to a different ball mark. On the changeovers he tried to intimidate his opponent by muttering things like "you know my shot was good." Or "that was the luckiest shot I have ever seen."

Sam's father was leaning on the fence on the side of the court of his opponent clapping and saying "good shot", even on Sam's balls that were clearly out. He groaned every time Sam hit into the net and yelled instructions to Sam. He even went so far as to call a foot-fault on the opponent.

Finally the opponent could no longer take it and asked for a roving umpire to come to the court. This really pissed Sam off, and on the first out call that the umpire overruled in the opponent's favor Sam slammed his racket to the ground. This drew a warning from the umpire. Sam lost it then. He started yelling at the umpire and his father joined in. Following the strict point penalty system, the umpire gave him a point penalty and when Sam persisted he awarded a game penalty to the opponent. Sam knew he would lose a match if he persisted, so he finally calmed down. After losing the first set in a tiebreak he couldn't take it any longer and smashed another racket. When the umpire reminded him that any other outburst would result in forfeiting the match, Sam got so angry that he completely lost focus and just wildly hit balls, losing the second set six-love. His father was beside himself, screaming obscenities at the umpire and the opponent as well as at Sam for being such a wimp. Meanwhile, Sam was cursing his opponent for being a cheat and the umpire for being biased against him. It was an ugly scene that solidified his reputation as a spoiled brat who would do anything necessary to win at all costs.

Chapter Four

Aunt Harriet began to sense the changes in Sam. She could feel his tension when he was around her, and she assumed it was a result of pressure from tennis. She was disturbed to see this wonderful game that can be such a vehicle for positive growth turning her favorite nephew in exactly the opposite direction. She knew she had to do something, or not only would Sam lose out in tennis, but she would lose the carefree, joyous nephew she had always loved. So she devised a two-pronged plan, one geared at Sam's father and one at Sam himself.

The first step was for her to attend several of Sam's matches and video tape them. She made sure to not only capture Sam on tape but also the actions of his father. Then she carefully edited the video to provide irrefutable evidence of the antics of each of them. When she was ready she first requested a meeting with Sam's father, saying she had some interesting observations about Sam's game. She had edited the tape to show Sam's mistakes on court, the father's reaction to it, and Sam's subsequent reaction and performance on the next few points.

They met at her house, and she escorted Sam's father into her private book-lined study. She insisted that neither of them say a word until the tape was played completely. When it was finished, and she could see that he had been squirming uncomfortably once he saw the gist of the tape, she asked him a simple question. "How do you think your presence at the match is affecting Sam's performance and enjoyment of the game?"

Although his normal nature was to become very defensive and even belligerent whenever faced with the slightest criticism of his actions, in this case he had no defense. "I guess it's putting too much pressure on him. He seems to be uptight and afraid to make mistakes.

He seems focused on winning at all costs, even if that means cheating and not playing his natural style." He admitted meekly as he squirmed in his chair.

"Do you love Sam?" Harriet inquired softly.

"I love Sam more than life itself," he said. "I would give my life for him. That's why I thought I should give him all the support possible to achieve his dreams in tennis."

Harriet sat in her old chair that was covered with a beautiful quilt and looked at him with real love in her eyes but a firm determination in her jaw. She held silence for a moment before asking, "Would you ever do anything to hurt him?"

"Of course, I would never intentionally hurt him. Yet you're showing me now that this is exactly what I'm doing. How is it that the complete opposite of what I intended is happening?" His question sounded sincere.

"Well," Harriet replied, "it looks like you've had a shift in your awareness by watching these tapes and recognizing the results of your actions. If you truly love Sam as much as you say you do, you're going to have to make some changes in your overall approach to him and his tennis."

"What do you suggest?' he replied.

"You first have to find out whether or not you can control your reactions to his play during a match," she said. "Why don't you attend his next couple matches but sit far away from the court where you can still be aware of the action yet he can't see or hear you." She laughed when she saw his grimace.

"It will be hard," he said, giving her the slightest smile.

"You can do it," she said. "Let's meet in two weeks to discuss what happened."

"Okay," he said, "I'll try it."

Two weeks later Sam's father admitted, "I don't think I can control my emotions at his matches. I want him to win so badly I can't stand to see him miss."

"Did you try the deep breathing exercises I suggested to help you stay more relaxed and focused?" Harriet asked.

"Yes, and they helped, but I still got too uptight and couldn't keep from gasping when he made a mistake. But he seemed to be playing much better when I wasn't sitting right on top of the court. I guess you were right about the negative impact my presence has on him. So what do I do?"

"You have to promise to never go to another of Sam's matches until he specifically asks you to attend."

He bolted out of his chair when he heard this, but Harriet didn't give him a chance to interrupt.

"Second, you can only ask him three questions when he returns home after any match or practice. One, 'Did you give your 100% effort throughout the match?' Two, 'Did you enjoy your time on court?' Three, 'What did you learn at practice or in the match that you can work to improve for the future?' "

"Wait a minute," he interrupted with a scowl on his face.

"No, you wait" Harriet responded as she adjusted her ever-present hat. "There's more. You are not to discuss scores, opponents, strategies, or rankings with him unless he specifically requests you to. Let his coaches do all of the coaching, goal setting, tournament planning and all other aspects that they are trained to handle and you are not. You need to focus on being a father who has unconditional love for his son regardless of what may transpire on the tennis court. Your job is to provide all of the monetary, educational, and travel assistance he requires while providing important emotional support. Be sure to hug him at least three times a day and tell him how much you love him. I know that's not your natural style, but you have to make some changes in your own mindset and behavior if you truly love your son as you claim to."

"Wow," Sam's father replied. "Do you mean I can never attend any of his matches in person until he asks me? Even if he becomes a professional, you mean I can't attend in person and have to watch him on TV?"

"Yep," Harriet replied. "That's what it means. Not until you are specifically requested by Sam can you ever attend one of his matches. Is that clear? Do we have a deal?"

Chapter Five

Lying in his Wimbledon hotel room and thinking about his father, Sam suspected that the sudden shift in his behavior had something to do with Aunt Harriet, but he had never known for sure. He had realized that his father no longer attended matches and restricted his commentary at home to just a few purposeful questions. His mother had started accompanying him to matches from then on. She had been very supportive and bore the burden of traveling with him, but she was never really emotionally involved in the matches. She simply wanted to see her son happy and doing what he loved. Now Sam realized that his father had never been in the audience at any of his matches. He had always felt that it was because his father's heart couldn't handle the pressure of the match. It finally struck him that his father had sacrificed his desire to be personally at matches in order to give Sam the best chance to get winning results. On a whim, Sam called Aunt Harriet, knowing that it was evening for her even though it was three in the morning where he was.

"Hi, Aunt Harriet. Did you see the match on TV?" Sam asked.

"Yes, of course." She replied. "I have never missed a TV match of yours in your entire career. I would never think of not tuning in on your most important one."

"Well," Sam said, "I want you to miss the telecast of the final. I want you to witness it in person from the players box. I want Father to be there as well, since you two have had the biggest influence in my success. Do you know what it would take to get him to come to the final?"

After getting over her initial shock, Aunt Harriet replied, "If you want me there for the final I'm happy to be there for you. As far as your father is concerned, all you have to do is ask him to come. That's what he's been waiting for all these years. He's still concerned that you think that if he's at the match you'll tighten up and find a way to lose. He loves you too much to have ever forced himself into that position, since the early days of your career."

"It sounds like you might have had something to do with his decision, Aunt Harriet."

"Well, I admit I had a talk with him. But the decision was his, once he realized how he could best express his love for you."

"You're amazing. I never thought my dad would accept advice from anyone."

"I'm sure it would be the proudest moment of his life to see the final in person. But you have to be certain it would have a positive and not a negative impact on your performance. You have to make certain in your own mind and heart that even with your father and me there you will remain focused on the task at hand and allow no distractions to prevent you from playing your best during the match. You have shown you can play with complete mindfulness, and this will be your ultimate test of the trust you carry within yourself."

As soon as Sam heard the word mindfulness he was immediately transported back to that essential time of transformation he had undergone in his game and as a human being, going from playing mind games to playing with mindfulness. He quickly thanked Aunt Harriet, asked her to let him know when her plane will arrive, and told her how much he loved and appreciated what an incredibly powerful influence she had been in his life. Then he hung up and sat remembering how Aunt Harriet had helped him overcome his horrible habits on court.

After finishing her work with Sam's father, Harriet had prepared a similar video (she called it a self-awareness video) of Sam during his matches. In his case, she had edited together numerous examples of him playing mind games with his opponent as well as his temper tantrums and nervous play. She linked them together to show the negative impact his tantrums had on his playing of the next few points. Like with his father, she made Sam sit silently through the entire presentation. When it was over she told him to sit in complete stillness for fifteen minutes to simply digest what he had seen and contemplate his actions. Those were the longest fifteen minutes of Sam's short life. He went through a huge range of emotions, from anger at Aunt Harriet, to disgust at himself, to pity towards his opponents, to hating the game of tennis and loathing what kind of person it had turned him into.

Finally, Aunt Harriet broke the interminable silence by asking the simple yet profound question, "What did you learn about yourself?"

Sam started slowly, unable to find the words to express the emotions he felt. As he tentatively began to describe how he felt he broke into tears. He hadn't cried since his favorite dog, Penny, died two years before, but now he broke down and sobbed uncontrollably. Aunt Harriet simply handed him a box of tissues and gave him the space to completely allow everything to come out. She didn't try to comfort or make him feel better. She simply let him feel all the pain that had suddenly burst to the surface. She knew this was the best way for him to purge the demons he felt inside his body and mind. She wanted him to clear his heart completely so he would be free of the past and able to make the necessary shift in his life.

After what had seemed like another eternity of crying, Sam wiped his tears and began to speak. "Aunt Harriet, I don't want to be the person on that video any more. Tennis isn't worth me becoming a complete jerk like I know I've been. I want to be the kind of person you have always seen me as. I want you to be proud of me as a loving, compassionate and aware person, not some spoiled tennis prima donna who only cares about himself and his wins on the tennis court. Can you help me make that change?"

That was the question Aunt Harriet had been preparing for. She said, "For the last year or so you've tried to win matches by playing a variety of mind games. That's a shortcut that will never lead to success. You've just seen what it does to your game, and more importantly to your heart. You no longer enjoy the game because you're consumed only with winning or losing. If you want to continue playing and start enjoying the game again you're going to have to switch from mind games to playing mindful tennis."

"What is mindful tennis?" Sam asked, twirling a lock of his hair nervously in his fingers.

"That's what you'll have to discover for yourself," Aunt Harriet replied. "Are you sure you want to play positive tennis?"

"Of course," Sam replied immediately.

"Then I'll make you a deal," she said. "I'll help you do that in the next two weeks, but you have to agree to do all the homework I assign you. It can be done in the time you normally spend practicing tennis, because I want you to take two weeks off and not hit another ball during that time."

"Wait a minute," Sam retorted. "How can I not practice for two weeks? My game will be the pits, and everyone else will pass me."

"Do you trust me?" Harriet said.

"Yes, I trust you, but you aren't my coach."

"Do you trust me in matters of your mind and your heart?"

"Yes. No question there."

"Well it's your mind and your heart that need a lot more time and dedication at this point than your tennis shots. I'll bet you a hot fudge sundae that your game will improve more in the next two weeks than it has in the past two months. Deal?"

"Deal," Sam said. "When do we start?"

"There's no time like the present," she said. "Today's assignment is to write down a list of all of the mind games you've ever played with an opponent. Think of why you used them, then list how you felt while using them and what the result of using them was, both in terms of game results and how it made you feel about yourself."

Sam looked like he had just run into a brick wall.

"To help you prepare for this task I'll give you the first lesson in mindfulness. Sit comfortably but erect. Now breathe deeply through your nose. As you do this put your hand on your stomach and feel the stomach moving in and out. Don't allow your shoulders to move up and down. Now feel yourself becoming more and more relaxed. Close your eyes and just focus on the air coming in and out of your nose. Feel the way the breath connects you with your entire environment. Feel how it makes you feel like you are connected with the vastness of the universe."

Over the course of the next two weeks Harriet had Sam spend three hours a day thinking about, writing about and practicing mindfulness. She had him write an article for the regional tennis magazine titled "From mind games to mindfulness." She taught him concentration practices, meditation, breathing exercises, use of positive affirmations and visualization skills. She worked on his visualization until he could concentrate long enough to see himself playing a complete match in his mind, always winning and constantly playing the way he wanted to play. Other times he would visualize himself in a tough match and see himself handling the challenges with poise and confidence. She also taught him how to consciously connect to the higher power of the universe, and how to trust that he had that power within himself.

At the end of the two weeks, Sam was eager to return to the tennis court. When he did, his fellow players immediately noticed the change. It seemed he was walking taller with a calm self-assurance. It was a far cry from the cocky arrogant walk he had developed previously. As soon as he started to hit it seemed like every ball was struck cleanly and would rocket off the sweet spot of the racket with the distinctive popping sound that the pros had. His intensity in going for every ball and hitting it as well as possible was balanced by the effortless way he seemed to move about the court and strike the ball with graceful power. The most amazing thing was that when he made the occasional mistake, instead of throwing his racket in disgust he would actually smile, give a little nod, and refocus immediately on the next point. He was so concentrated on every point, regardless of the score or what had happened on the previous point, that soon he was easily winning matches against players who had given him trouble before. Although his fellow trainees tried to play all kinds of mind games to throw him off, Sam seemed to be impervious to any attempts to cheat or upset him. He just serenely continued to hit incredible shots one after another, no matter what the situation was. He was playing with joy and creativity that was beyond anything he had ever felt in his life. At the end of one week, he called Aunt Harriet and simply said, "Let's go out for ice cream. I owe you a hot fudge sundae."

Back in London, after talking with Aunt Harriet, Sam had been wrestling with the dilemma of whether or not to invite his father to attend the final. On one hand he knew that it would mean the world to his father to see him competing in the finals of Wimbledon. At the same time he was still concerned that the long buried feelings of fear and unconscious pressure he had felt under his father's gaze could return and cause him to lose the match. He knew his father would feel guilty if he lost and it could crush him. Sam decided there was only one way to know for sure what he should do. It was now almost four in the morning, but Sam sat up erect in his bed and began to meditate, as he had done thousands of times over the past fifteen years. He meditated, prayed, and asked the universe to guide him in what he should do. This method had always given him great comfort and peace of mind. Especially over the past six months it had really taken on a new level, and he felt he was receiving direct guidance in every decision he had to make.

While meditating he suddenly received a very clear answer. Of course he should invite his father. Sam had to trust the strength within himself to overcome any previous mental issues he had experienced. His love for his father outweighed any other consideration. He saw clearly that winning and losing the final was no longer that important. What was important was the growth that Sam had experienced through his journey as a tennis professional. The final test of that growth was his ability to extend complete forgiveness to his father and offer him an opportunity to feel the ultimate level of joy in his life. He now understood how much his father loved him and how much he had sacrificed on his behalf in so many ways. The only way he could even attempt to repay that was to allow his father to see in person what a tremendous individual and competitor he had become. He knew his father would be proud of his conduct and his level of passion for life and tennis, regardless of the ultimate outcome of the match.

Sam picked up the phone and dialed. "Hi, Dad, it's me. I love you. Did you watch the semis on TV?"

His father's first reaction was that of shock. "Sam. It must be about four in the morning. Why are you still awake? Don't you need to get some sleep? Of course, I watched the semis. Have I ever missed any of your televised matches? You were fantastic."

"Dad, I would love nothing more than for you to be there for me in the players' box during the final. Please book your flight now. I'll take care of everything else. Will you come?"

"Son, I don't know how to tell you this, but ever since you were twelve I've felt I was the reason you lost matches and behaved badly on court. I knew the pressure I put on you to win was too much to handle. Perhaps you know now that Aunt Harriet helped me realize this, and I promised to stay away from your matches. When I saw the immediate improvement in your game, I knew that if I ever came to another match you might lose and I would blame myself for it. I could never live with the thought that I had caused you to lose the most important contest of your life. Your success and happiness means more to me than anything in life, and I can't risk jeopardizing that out of fatherly pride and arrogance."

"I understand." Sam replied, holding back a tear as he felt his father's genuine love come through his words. "Aunt Harriet just told me about the promise you made to her. What you don't know is that at that time she also spent two weeks teaching me how to trust my inner strength and learn to play with mindfulness. That transformation in my attitude is what caused the sudden leap in my playing success, not the fact that you weren't at my matches. Throughout my entire career I thought you stayed away because your heart couldn't bear the pressure of me playing. Yet no matter how often I won, I always felt a little something lacking in my happiness because you weren't there to share it with me."

"My heart only wanted you to be happy, and I never want to feel that I prevented you from achieving your dreams," Sam's father said softly.

"Dad, I want to be able to feel absolute joy when that match ends, regardless of the result. I want you to be able to express your pride in me as your son in front of the entire world. If the scoreboard ends up in the other guy's favor it won't be your fault, nor will it be mine. It will only be because I faced a better opponent that day. I will have given my finest effort possible and will have no regrets regardless of the outcome. The only regret I could possibly have is to not have you there to share the crowning achievement of my career. If I win the match and can't share an immediate hug with you, there will always be something missing. Please Dad. I'm asking you to please come see me in the finals. Actually I'm begging you to be there, for your sake and for mine."

There was nothing but silence at the other end of the line. Yet Sam could hear muffled sobs and could visualize the tears in his father's eyes. Sam had never seen his tough father cry, but he knew at this moment years of repressed emotions were pouring through his father's heart. He could feel the pride his father felt for him. He knew he had become the man his father had always prayed he would become. Finally, after blowing his nose a couple times and clearing his throat, his father spoke. "My dear Sam. You know I'll do anything you ever ask me to do. You have offered me the greatest gift of my life. I love you so much and am so proud of you, Son."

"Thanks, Dad. You've just given me the most incredible gift. I can already see you sitting in the box between Mom and Aunt Harriet. I love you Dad, more than you can know. And Dad, don't forget to bring your raincoat and umbrella. It rains a lot in London, but it won't on the day of the final. It will be the most beautiful day of our lives."

After hanging up with his father, Sam felt relief flow through his body. He had now overcome the final barrier to his complete happiness. He knew his father had been the missing link in his career. He knew his father had loved and supported him from afar, but he wanted to experience that pride in the present, in the flesh. Now he knew the final would be a complete and amazing experience regardless of the outcome. He was so wired he knew he couldn't get back to sleep no matter how much he needed it. He realized sleep was not going to give him the energy he would need for the final. That would have to come from within. He planned to get some extra sleep during the day, so he got up to prepare for what he thought would be a relaxing recovery day.

How wrong he was. As soon as he switched on his iPhone he saw he had over a hundred SMS messages waiting for him. He had even more emails in his inbox. One of the other promises he had made to himself was that he would always be accessible to the media, fans, and friends and would personally reply to every SMS and email within twenty-four hours. That had been fairly easy when he was a relatively unknown player, although he had attracted a lot of fans and friends due to his exuberant personality and style of play. Now he realized he may have to modify his rule a bit or he would spend the whole day on his computer. He quickly wrote a generic response thanking people for their best wishes and assuring them that he would hold their energy in his heart and give his best in the final. Then he sent out a blanket SMS to all who had written. Sometimes technology was a real time waster, but good use of it could sure save a lot of time sometimes. He put the same message on auto respond to his emails as well.

When he started to sift through them he realized that at least a dozen of the messages were from members of the press wanting an exclusive interview with him. His was such an unexpected rise to the top that everyone wanted to get the scoop on what had changed to allow him to reach such a height after so many years of struggle in anonymity on the tour. He wasn't ready to share that secret with the media just yet, but he knew how expert they were at twisting things around and being persistent and sneaky enough to trick even the most guarded secrets out of the interviewee. He responded individually to each one of them saying that he would be available for interviews between eleven and noon that day. It would not be a formal press conference, but that would be the only time he would be available to the press. Whereas before he would have begged for any amount of press attention, this time it felt good to be in control of his time and put them on the defensive. He knew he had to protect his time and his focus if he were to be prepared for the final step in achieving his dream.

Chapter Six

After a quick shower, Sam sat down for what had become the most important part of his day, his time of meditation. He had become quite proficient at clearing his mind of thoughts and being able to only focus on visualizing playing a perfect match. On this day he couldn't hold back the flood of memories of his past that had started during the night. His thoughts returned to his formative years and his big break when he was offered a scholarship at a prestigious tennis academy.

It had been a difficult choice for Sam. He got very attached to his favorite coaches and always had trouble leaving them. It first happened when Jay left when Sam was twelve. Roland had gotten very jealous of the success Jay was having and especially the amazing rapport he had with the kids. Instead of being happy to have such a coach on his team, he took it as a personal affront to his ego. He ultimately told Jay he would have to go, not realizing that most of the players would leave his program and go with Jay. But Jay didn't want to create that kind of pressure on the kids, and he received a very good offer from a facility in a neighboring state so he moved too far for the kids to come with him.

Sam was moved into Roland's top group where he was competing with kids four and five years older. After discussing it with his parents he had insisted on two things from Roland. First, that Roland make him work harder than all the other players on every drill, and second that Roland never talk to him about his technique but allow him to use his own style. At first Roland was resistant, but he recognized Sam's talent and knew he had something special that could potentially bring prestige to his program, so he agreed.

The first year was barely tolerable and that was when Sam's father had made his ill-fated attempt at coaching. But after Sam's breakthrough with Aunt Harriet he was also blessed with a new assistant coach, Peter. Although his relationship with Peter wasn't the same as with Jay, Peter also had a very positive attitude toward the players and made the game fun. He knew how to make even the toughest and most challenging drills and physical fitness training so engaging and fun that the kids never wanted to stop and ended up working twice as hard as they ever imagined they could. Sam loved being on Peter's court, and when the offer of the scholarship came, he had to make a tough choice with a lot of things to consider.

In his local program he was now the best player so he was not being pushed on a daily basis. He knew consistently strong competition was essential to his continued progress, and that was a major enticement for going to the academy. It would also take the burden off his parents, paying not only for his coaching but also his tournament travel expenses. He would soon start playing ITF junior tournaments in addition to national tournaments, so the travel requirements would only be increasing. The move made sense on many levels, yet there were many things holding him back. He would have to leave his school and attend a private academy school that was geared toward athletes. He would have to leave Peter and the friends he had grown up playing with. Most difficult would be leaving his parents as well as Aunt Harriet. How would he handle being away from their stabilizing influence in his life? He knew he could always count on them to give him unconditional love, and the affection and support they gave him was a big part of who he was.

Finally, he and his parents, along with Peter and Aunt Harriet, decided that he had to look to his future and take the step that would give him the best chance to pursue his dream. This was a tremendous opportunity to go to the famous academy where the top juniors in the world went for competition. It was also an opportunity to rub shoulders with the numerous professional players who visited there regularly to train. Although Sam was not excited about the move, his mind said that he had to give it a shot. So he said goodbye to his friends and family and boarded the plane for a new world and a new life.

From the moment he arrived at the academy, Sam felt in his heart that it was not the right place for him. It was more like a boot camp than a place for nurturing eager young athletic talent. His first greeting was more like an induction, simply giving him his equipment and telling him where to live. At least they didn't force him to shave off all his hair like the army would. His roommate barely grunted an acknowledgement, and obviously saw him just as another competitor trying to take his spot at the top. The school had the same feeling. There was very little friendship. Everyone was focused only on getting through the syllabus as quickly as possible so they could return to the court.

On court was another matter. There was absolutely none of the fun games and drills that Sam had learned from Jay and Peter. This was simply drilling, drilling, and more drilling. Hitting thousands of fed balls every morning. It was run and hit, run and hit, then return to the line. There was virtually no instruction, just the exhortation to hit harder and deeper on every ball. At least they weren't trying to change his style of play, as the coaches seemed to be more like ball machines to feed balls rather than mentors who were there to inspire and guide the students. The afternoons were reserved for match play. These were not the handicap type matches where limitations were placed on at least one of the players to force them to work on a specific part of their game and test it under match pressure. These were all cut-throat ladder matches that determined whether or not you moved up to the next group. Everything at the academy was based on what group you were in. The higher you went, the more respect you received and the greater number of perks and freedom you were given.

Every newcomer was placed in the bottom group, regardless of their ranking, scholarship or previous results. This allowed Sam to win a lot of easy matches and move up quickly. It also dulled his competitive instincts as he often had near beginners on his court whose weak strokes and undeveloped work ethic started to affect his own. Fortunately, he moved up quickly enough to avoid being drawn into lowering his standard of play. As he moved up the ladder he began to feel some of the pressure he had previously felt from his father, and it was starting to bring back some of his old habits. Cheating was rampant in the matches. Gamesmanship here was a 24/7 affair with every interaction with fellow players seeming to be geared toward showing how confident you were and making the others feel inferior. As much as he tried to remain true to his promise to Aunt Harriet, he found himself being drawn into the culture of mind games that permeated the campus.

He tried to make time to meditate, but the schedule was packed with at least six hours a day on court along with school and two hours a day of physical training. There was barely time to eat before falling in bed exhausted at the end of every day. There was never a full day off, only a half day off on Sunday when everyone was forced to go to a boring church service followed by whatever movie was playing at the local mall. Sam would have given anything for just an hour a week to be able to get out in nature, run through a forest or simply enjoy listening to the chirping of the birds or the rustling of leaves in the woods. But this academy had no place for recovery or rejuvenation. It was like a factory churning out hitters of the tennis ball. If you made it, great. If you got burned out along the way, no problem, there were ten more lined up to take your place in the pursuit of their dream. Sam began to wonder how his dream had so quickly turned into a nightmare.

His only solace was the weekly phone call he was able to make home. Since he had only one call and limited time, he alternated weeks between his parents and Aunt Harriet.

Sam's parents were always positive and supportive, urging him to look at the positive aspects of being at the academy and insisting that he eat well and get enough rest to remain healthy. Aunt Harriet's approach was somewhat different. Her typical conversation would go something like this.

"I don't want to hear any more complaining about the environment you're in. What are you doing to affect your environment? Those who are weak and never achieve much always blame their circumstances or their parents for their lack of success. Those who are successful never let the environment dictate their attitude or their accomplishments. They see all difficult circumstances as opportunities to test their courage and enable them to become stronger in the process."

"What do you suggest I do?" Sam asked as he looked over his shoulder to see if any of the other players could overhear his conversation.

"Are you meditating regularly?"

"No, there is no time for meditation."

"Why don't you ask them to create a group meditation session? It sounds like that is what all the kids there need most."

"Remember, you suggested that last month. I did ask the head coach if a meditation class is possible. He simply laughed at me and called me a wimp. He said that was my problem, that I was soft and not tough enough to compete with the others."

"Okay. Now we know the mentality you are dealing with." Aunt Harriet replied with just a hint of disgust at the small-mindedness of the coaches. "I'm proud of you for trying, even if you got shot down. If you can't change the environment then you have to change your internal perspective. What time do you go to sleep and wake up?"

"Lights out is at ten and wake-up call is at five-thirty," Sam said.

"Would it be possible to meditate for ten minutes just after lights out and get up ten minutes early to meditate before getting up for the day?" She asked.

"I guess I could try it." Sam replied. "Wouldn't it cause me to lose sleep and affect my energy levels?"

"You'll have to test that for yourself. It's my experience that most people find the energy they gain from meditation is equal to getting double that amount of sleep. It really is magical. Try it and let me know. Then if you can find another five or ten minutes during the day to close your eyes and center yourself, it can help you remain positive when dealing with the negativity you face. Let me know how it goes."

It was tough at first for Sam to stay awake to meditate before going to bed and getting up early was a real challenge, but he gradually got used to it. Then he began to look forward to that time as his personal rejuvenation time. He even tried to close his eyes right after lunch and regain the quiet space in his mind. Soon he began to notice that he was less nervous and didn't get as upset as before when he was cheated in matches or hassled by the others in the locker room. Although this habit made life tolerable for him, Sam still wasn't happy and certainly didn't feel he could take another four or five years there. He told his parents he would be coming home at the end of the year, and would decide whether or not it was worth it to continue to pursue his dream of a career in tennis or just begin to focus completely on his studies and become a doctor or an engineer.

One thing Sam really enjoyed about the time he spent at the academy was the tournaments they played in. Sam always enjoyed traveling and meeting new people. It was also a relief to escape what he saw as the prison walls of the academy. The bus rides were tough, as he didn't join the others in their arrogant banter. He preferred to plug in his iPod headsets and listen to music that boosted his spirits and gave him energy.

In the last two months of the year they flew to a couple events in a different part of the country. Sam's first opponent in the first tournament was a player named Joe. As they shook hands, Joe smiled broadly, looked Sam in the eye and gave a warm and firm handshake. The lack of arrogance is what Sam first noticed. Sam took that as a sign of weakness and breathed a sigh of relief that he had an easy first round match.

As they warmed up, Joe seemed too polite and almost fragile to put up much of a fight, and besides, he didn't blast every ball with power like the guys in the academy. Sam settled in and knew he was going to enjoy this easy first-round match. But once the match started, Sam found he was struggling to win points. No matter how much power he threw at him, Joe found a way to return the balls. Joe's serve didn't look powerful, but it was consistent, well-placed and seemed to always fool Sam and force him to hit a weak return that Joe would smoothly hit for a winner in the open court. Even Sam's biggest serves or winning forehands would somehow come back. He felt himself getting frustrated.

After going down love-three, Sam picked up the pace and started going for winners on every shot. He was determined that no retriever would ever beat him. But the more he tried to hit great shots the more he started to make mistakes. After losing the first set 6-1, Sam decided he would have to change tactics. He started to play mind games to throw Joe off. He made a couple blatantly wrong line calls. On the second bad call, Joe asked "Are you sure?" and smilingly accepted Sam's lie of yes. The same thing happened on the next three bad calls Sam made. No outburst from Joe. He didn't even call for a roving linesperson, just a persistent "Are you sure?" with no argument when Sam answered yes. Worse yet, Joe's concentration didn't get affected by the bad calls. In fact it seemed to improve. Even the dozen kids that had been cheering for Joe didn't get angry at what they knew were bad line calls. They didn't come and stand by the lines as Sam's father used to do when he knew Sam was being cheated.

Sam tried every trick in the book: stalling, calling the wrong score, deliberately playing Joe's long first serves. Nothing seemed to affect Joe's politeness, his concentration or his game. Sam was going crazy. He started throwing his racket after missed shots, and all his frustrations came out. How could he lose to this guy? But lose he did 6-1, 6-1. He barely shook Joe's hand and stormed off the court in disgust. Boy, did he hear about it from his fellow academy students. They all berated him for losing so badly to a nobody. Sam couldn't bear it any longer, so he went off by himself to think. Fortunately, there was a beautiful nature park right beside the tournament site.

Sam sat down beside a brook and closed his eyes to listen to the birds singing. It had been a long time since he has been in nature and it made it easy to go into a deep meditation. He almost felt the presence of Aunt Harriet. She seemed to be telling him what a great opportunity he just had to learn about himself. Hadn't his opponent just played the way he would like to play, with mindfulness and positive concentration? Hadn't the results proven that this was more important than power and arrogance? The more he connected with her the more he became ashamed of the way he had behaved. What was the purpose of his anger and mind games if it hadn't helped him win? Instead he just felt like a loser and a jerk. He didn't like that feeling. In fact, he started to hate the way he was performing on the court, in his game as well as his attitude. He felt Aunt Harriet gently urging him to make friends with Joe and find out what his secret was.

After soaking up a few more minutes of nature and remembering how much he loved its soothing affect on him, Sam went looking for Joe. He found him with his mates cheering for one of their players. Ironically, that player was in the process of handing one of Joe's academy mates a beating almost as bad as Sam had experienced. At the changeover, Sam nervously approached Joe and said he wanted to apologize for how badly he had behaved during the match. Joe accepted with a gracious smile.

"I appreciate your courage in coming to apologize. I understand the pressure you're under to win at all costs. I was expecting the bad calls, since we were forewarned that everyone at your academy cheats. Somehow you don't seem like the rest of them. Why don't you join our group after the match and get to know everyone?"

Sam was thrown aback by Joe's honesty and warmth. He had never met another good junior who seemed so genuine.

"Are you sure the others wouldn't mind, especially after seeing what a jerk I was during our match?" Sam asked incredulously, as he fiddled with the racket he had smashed during the match.

"Sure, I can feel that at heart you belong with us much more than with your academy mates. You'll fit in fine with us." Joe's sincerity came through his deep blue eyes.

Although he felt like a bit of a traitor, he joined Joe's group and soon discovered that all of them were almost as nice and friendly as Joe. And many of them had earned similar results on the court. Most of the players from Sam's academy had lost in the early rounds, but they had to stay the rest of the week to play doubles and practice for the tournament the next week. Sam was glad, as it gave him time to spend more time in the park as well as get to know the members of Joe's group. The serenity of the nature park seemed to clear Sam's head. He began to notice the difference between the attitudes of the players of his academy and those of Joe's. He also realized how differently the coaches treated them. Instead of yelling and berating the players for not working hard enough, Joe's coach was always encouraging, laughing, and asking them questions to make them think. He made it fun for them, and they seemed to respond by working harder than ever to keep up with the rest of the group. Most important, they all seemed to enjoy each other's company and supported each other in every way. They were all great friends and knew how to reach out and make friends with others. By the end of the week, Sam felt like they were all his friends. It felt good.

Chapter Seven

Sam was delighted to learn that the next tournament was going to be held at Joe's academy. What a wonderful coincidence! He would have a chance to see this magical place where these positive players were being created. But as he drove onto the grounds he was disappointed. Instead of rows and rows of courts of all surfaces, with huge banners everywhere and a fresh corporate look like his academy, this place almost looked like someone's old family farm. Just one modest sign let visitors know they had arrived. The twelve hard courts were not well landscaped, although they were clean and everything was very neat. The clubhouse was simple and small. The most disappointing was the weight room. Instead of row after row of the latest, shiniest equipment, this place had a bunch of bands connected to a grillwork that covered one whole wall of the almost empty gym. They had a few pieces of nice cardio equipment: treadmills, ellipticals, and bikes, but the only piece of weight equipment was a leg press. There was no big cafeteria, just one huge oval dining table that almost reminded Sam of the Knights of the Round Table at Camelot. Everything seemed so simple and sparse, yet there was a feeling of peacefulness and clean energy that Sam began to pick up on. It was the same with the dormitories they were staying in, simple, yet very functional. With so many tournament players coming in they didn't have enough space to house everyone. Joe asked Sam if he would like to stay in his room. Joe said he would be happy to sleep on an air mattress on the floor and give Sam his bed. Sam was blown away by this gesture.

Sam's academy coach couldn't believe the accommodations were so rustic. He immediately announced that his players would be moving to a hotel at a town twenty miles away. Sam firmly told him that he had a room here and wanted to stay with Joe. The coach went berserk.

"What are you, some kind of traitor? I've seen you hanging out with these guys all week. Are you going to start rooting for them against your own academy mates?"

Taking a deep breath, Sam calmly replied, "You know, I just might. When have my academy mates ever cheered for me?"

With that the coached stormed out slapping his cap against his thigh. "Do what you like, you loser. At least it will save us some money."

After hearing that exchange Joe said, "Wow. How have you been able to put up with that kind of attitude? It must be tough."

"Yeah" Sam answered. "It's been the most difficult year of my life. I'm leaving at the end of the year. I'll probably go back home and give up the dream of becoming a tennis professional."

"Oh no. Don't do that. You can be a great player. You have all the weapons to make it on the pro circuit. Once you learn to focus your mind on the positive and learn to play with strategy instead of sheer power you will be awesome. Why don't you join our academy here? Come on, let me show you the rest of the campus."

As Sam was shown the rest of the campus (that actually had been an old family farm) he began to get the feeling he had found his new home. There was a nice little forest with great walking trails and a stream running through it. When they reached a beautiful meadow with an area of neatly trimmed grass that Joe described as their meditation space, Sam was hooked. He knew this is where he belonged. "Who can I talk to about getting a scholarship?"

"I'm so glad you want to go here," Joe said, his smile even more radiant than normal. "Let me introduce you to coach Andy and his wife, Tina. They're very busy organizing the tournament right now, but let's see if they can spare a few minutes to talk to you"

As they went through the open door of the modest office, Joe introduced Sam to Coach Andy and Tina. Sam was shocked when Andy greeted him with a huge smile and followed a strong handshake with a warm hug. Tina did the same.

"Welcome, Sam. Joe has told us what a fantastic player you are. It seems like you two have become very close friends in such a short time. Welcome to our academy."

"Thank you," Sam started hesitatingly. "I sure didn't play great against Joe. He killed me, even though I was a complete jerk. What amazed me was that he wasn't fazed by any of my antics. He welcomed me as a friend even after the way I treated him. It's been great to get to know your players. They're the kind of people I'd like to be around on a regular basis. I'm very interested in knowing more about you and this academy you have built."

"Well, Sam," Andy began as he touched Sam on the shoulder. "We like to think of it more like a family than an academy. I've had a passion for tennis since I was young, but it pains me to see so many so-called academies that are destroying the spirit of this wonderful game in the name of wins and rankings. We have a completely different philosophy here. It certainly isn't a place for every player. In fact we're quite selective about who we allow to come. If the player doesn't have a positive attitude, or if we don't think they can develop a good attitude in the right environment, then we don't accept them. We're not interested in recruiting top-ranked players. All too often they have tremendous ego issues. Instead we prefer to select players who have a great work ethic and who we think will thrive in the unique atmosphere we've created."

Andy drew Sam's attention to the window with a panoramic view of the courts and the forest in the background.

"It takes a very strong person to not be affected by the environment they're in," Coach Andy said. "I sense you have a pure heart, and it saddens me to see what's happened to you because you have not been in the right place. Let's use this week as a test to find out whether it would be the right fit for you here. Since you're staying with us, I'll ask our players to treat you as if you're already part of our team. I hope you'll reciprocate and support them as if you were one of us. Let's see what happens to you on court when you're part of a loving and supportive atmosphere."

"You really want me to act like part of your team this week?" Sam replied with shock in his voice.

"Don't you already feel like you're at home here with our players?" Andy asked, seemingly reading Sam's thoughts.

Sam loved the idea of being accepted into this new family of friends, and he already felt a great respect for Coach Andy and Tina. He knew he would have to be on his best behavior to be accepted, so he vowed to do his best. He wanted to talk to his parents about a possible shift in academies and see what they thought. He hesitantly brought up the subject of fees with Andy.

"If I were to be accepted here, I know my parents would be interested in knowing what the financial arrangements would be. I have a full scholarship at the other academy and they would want to know if the same arrangement would be possible here."

"That's a very important question," Andy replied, moving across the room to his desk. "Whenever making an important decision it's always good to be clear about the financial side of things right from the start. We give scholarships, but only to kids who have fantastic attitudes and come from homes that could never provide the opportunity for them to pursue their dreams. Even if they don't have what it takes to become a professional, if we can help them develop great leadership skills and create a wonderful life for themselves then we feel our gift to them has been worthwhile. For families who can afford it, we think it's important that they make the commitment to pay the full price in order to help us support those who are in less fortunate circumstances. In your case, tell your parents they would need to pay our full rates the first year."

Sam winced when he heard this, knowing how difficult it would be for his parents to handle that kind of financial burden.

"Don't worry" Andy responded, again seeming to read Sam's mind. "We have a system of incentives whereby you can help your parents reduce that burden in a number of ways. One is based on your attitude score that we evaluate every week. Another way is for you to do certain things to help others. You can help out with our projects in the slums, help with our wheelchair program, or several other volunteer options to share your knowledge with those less fortunate than you. In this way you're gaining valuable experience while showing your parents how much you appreciate their support by trying to relieve their payment somewhat. You can explain the system to them and see what they think about it. Meanwhile, I hope you can prove yourself worthy this week. We're all looking forward to having you become part of our family."

That week went by like a dream for Sam. In the first two rounds he played guys from his old academy that he had always lost to. With his new friends cheering him on, he defeated them both easily. After winning one more round he faced Joe in the semi-finals. The night before the match they joked around with each other about how important the match was and how they were going to cheat and do whatever it took to defeat the other. It was all in lighthearted fun. They had already become best of friends and no match could ever cause them to give up what they realized was a very special gift.

It was an incredible match. Players from Sam's current academy had come out in force to root against him, the traitor. Andy's academy students were rooting equally for Joe and Sam. Everyone was amazed at the quality of tennis they were witnessing. Both players were completely focused on every point. They were using an astonishing array of shots, creating angles and openings on the court that were seemingly impossible. Each point seemed like it had everything in it: power, finesse, drop shots, volleys, defensive miracles, and non-stop hustle.

Everyone watching was enthralled as the momentum swung back and forth. Joe took the first set 7-5, but Sam made a few adjustments to take the second 6-4. At 5-all in the third everyone sensed a tiebreak was in store. No one wanted the match to end, and they certainly didn't want either player to have to lose the match. They knew both of them were playing and acting like champions. They were playing with courage, taking bold risks yet it was intelligent tennis, always choosing a shot appropriate for the situation. Both had fantastic attitudes and actually overruled the umpire to give the opponent the point when they knew a wrong call had been made. They were clapping with genuine appreciation when the other made an unreturnable winner that had taken them by surprise. By the third set, everyone had forgotten who they were rooting for or against and were simply cheering for the most spectacular tennis they had seen in a long time.

The tiebreak stayed on serve until Sam reached match point with Joe serving at 6-7. Sam had been struggling with Joe's serve throughout the entire match. He knew this might be his only chance. He guessed that Joe would serve a hard one up the middle on the add court, a serve that had fooled Sam often on critical points. Sure enough the serve came there, and it was a beauty. It hit right in the corner and had Sam not anticipated it perfectly it would have been an ace. But Sam lunged out at the ball and got his racket on it. It had just enough pace to make it to the net, hit the top of the tape, and meekly drop onto Joe's side for a winner.

Both players were stunned, yet somehow they knew the only way that match could have ended was by a lucky fluke or divine intervention, whichever way you wanted to look at it. Once they both realized it was over they slowly seemed to emerge from the almost trancelike state in which they had both played the match. Joe jumped over the net and gave Sam a warm, sweaty hug, as the crowd cheered both players. Everyone knew they had just witnessed something special, and both Joe and Sam hoped it would be only the first of many opportunities they would have to battle each other to the finish and force each of them to discover shots, strategies and courage they never knew they had before.

Sam had never been happier in his life. His joy increased even more when he called home to tell his parents. They had spent the last few days working out their finances to see how they could pay for Sam's new academy. With some help from Aunt Harriet they were able to secure enough to pay for the first six months.

"Son, you have made us so proud, and we'll do whatever it takes to see you in a place where you're happy," his dad said. "We have only enough for six months, but we have complete faith in your ability to earn some scholarship credits, and we'll trust that the universe will provide whatever is lacking. We know this is the right step for you, and we're backing you all the way."

Sam couldn't hold back the flood of tears. "Dad, you've been so supportive during my entire career. Being here means more to me than anything in the world. It's where I belong and where I can truly pursue my dream. I'll do whatever it takes to make certain I can remain here as long as possible and take as much of the financial strain off you as I can. When I make it big on the circuit, I'll buy you anything you want."

"Thanks, Son," said his father. "You know money can't buy what I want most. That is your happiness and fulfillment. Now go out there and have fun in the final."

The final pitted Sam against the best player of his old academy. He was two groups ahead of Sam, so they had never really practiced or played against each other. He was one of the 'chosen ones' who got special attention and coaching from the director since he was touted to be a future number one player in the world. He had won seventy-five percent of the tournaments he had entered that year and was ranked number one in the country. Sam had always been intimidated by him, and he was a master at using his awesome size and power to take full advantage of that intimidation factor. This time the division in the cheering section couldn't have been more obvious. All the players from Sam's old academy were on one side while all from Andy's academy and any other players who were still around were on Sam's side. There was a fever pitch in the air as everyone was anticipating a supreme battle if Sam could reach the level of play he had displayed in the semis.

Instead the battle never developed. It was a one-sided affair, but not in the direction that rankings and past results would have predicted. Sam put on another masterful display of superbly orchestrated tennis that threw the opponent out of his rhythm. He appeared to be off balance when not allowed to be in his accustomed situation of dictating points from an offensive position. When the inevitable mind games were tried, along with bad line calls and racket throwing, Sam was a picture of composure. Nothing rattled his firm resolve to remain focused on the present. By the end of the match even his old academy mates were applauding Sam's shots. They couldn't believe this was the same player they had seen lose his temper and blow so many matches in the past. It was like he had completely transformed before their eyes in one week.

While accepting the winner's trophy, Sam insisted that Joe join him on the podium. "This is the true champion," Sam said, putting his arm around Joe. "I've learned more from him and gotten closer to him in the past two weeks than anyone in my life. If it weren't for a lucky net cord he would have won the final, not me. We've shared a room all week, we've shared great talks, and we'll share this trophy forever. I'm happy to announce that this academy will be my new home, and I look forward to sharing many more wonderful moments with Joe and with all of the amazing people here. Thank you so much, Coach Andy and Tina for not only putting on such a special tournament, but for creating this beautiful environment for budding tennis players to thrive in. Oh, I almost forgot. Did I pass the test for entrance into the academy?"

"Of course you have, Sam." Andy replied. He gave him a big hug as everyone cheered and some wiped tears from their eyes. "You've shown the attitude that we look for here. You'll be an excellent role model for all the other players and those to come in the future. Thanks for showing us such inspired tennis along with the ideal sportsmanship that's even more important. You're a most worthy champion of this tournament."

Chapter Eight

Sam didn't even return to his old academy. He felt like he was home. He just asked them to pack up his things and send them to him. It didn't take him long to settle into the routine at the academy. As he did he began to notice a number of differences in the way things were handled at this academy compared to his previous one. The first thing he noticed was how actively involved Andy and Tina were, not just on court but in the lives of each of the students. They didn't sit in some ivory tower and judge the talent but instead continually asked how players were feeling, how things were back home, what they thought was lacking in their lives or at the academy, and how positive their energy level was. Players felt very comfortable approaching any of the coaches at any time. Whether it was a question about technique, tactics or strategy on court, or fitness, nutrition or any other aspect of life, questions were always encouraged and answered with compassion and honesty.

The on-court experience was another huge contrast. There were a certain number of repetition drills to focus on technique and learning new shots. But they were all based on specific situations and shot combinations that were likely to occur during a match. They were almost never simply standing and hitting, but very dynamic with realistic feeding to simulate match conditions. In fact many of the feeding drills were much tougher than a match, as players would be forced to hit so many balls that they would be dead tired and their legs would be almost ready to collapse. Then the next fifteen or twenty balls would have to be hit well in order to end the drill. It taught the players to focus and hit their best shots even during the roughest stages of the match when their legs were rubbery. That is where matches are won and lost, so practicing under that pressure made the students mentally tough.

Although the drills were much more dynamic, the real difference was in the area of competition. They played matches at least twice a week, but there were an incredible variety of situational games played every day. These were used to bridge the gap between the conditions during drilling and real matches. They were very stimulating because they were fun and yet always had a purpose connected with the theme that was being worked on that day. Sometimes there was cooperative competition where two players hit cooperatively to reach a goal and outdo each of the other teams. Many of the games were limitation games where you had to play in a certain way or lose the point. For example, in one game you had to be inside the service line when you won the point in order to get credit for it. In another game both players had to remain inside the baseline the entire time and would lose the point if they stepped behind it. There were innumerable variations, but all served to help players be at ease competing in situations where they might be uncomfortable.

Even the matches themselves often had interesting twists. The superior player might be given a handicap, either in scoring or a limitation like only getting one serve. This kept the match close regardless of the disparity in age or level. In this way all the players in the academy played against almost all others. The idea was that you could gain benefit from playing against players much better than you to get accustomed to being on the defensive on a regular basis. You could also gain by playing against inferior opponents, as this was a time to practice new shots, new strategies and work on taking the risks needed to play dominating offensive tennis. There were serious ladder matches that increased in frequency before major tournaments, and these were staged to simulate exact tournament conditions.

The result of these consistently varied types of competition was that practices never got boring or too repetitive. The kids were constantly challenging themselves to experience new types of situations and learning to deal with them effectively. The purpose was always to increase awareness during the match and develop trust in your ability to respond to all challenges in the most appropriate way. Instead of daily cutthroat match play there was a spirit of teamwork and camaraderie. At the end of most practice sessions they would all gather to play a fun team game that often required unusual shots, but always brought the group together in the spirit of fun. That is what Sam enjoyed the most, that the game became fun and stimulating again. He was free to explore his own creativity and develop the flexibility to play almost any style of tennis. All the players were developing complete games as well as learning to think for themselves and cultivate strategies that would enable them to adapt to constantly changing match conditions. They were getting so strong mentally as well as physically that nothing they could face in a match could ever faze them.

The physical training was another huge difference. The emphasis was always on ways to make it as fun and engaging as possible. Many of the drills were turned into team competitions. Each student was assessed monthly, and a specific program was created to match their age and physical development. Care was always taken to not put too much stress on the body and always allow for adequate rest and recovery. All exercises were geared toward sport specific movements, not just building up bulky muscles. That's why bands were used regularly instead of weight machines. The trainers were just as fun and enthusiastic as all of the tennis coaches. Instead of demanding that the players push their bodies to the limit, they constantly asked them questions while helping them develop their own awareness of the body. If a player felt something was not right, they would either move to something different or cancel the session that day. By empowering the students to take responsibility for their own body and learning to trust their own intuition the kids actually took more pride in their physical development and created the understanding that would prepare them to remain physically fit for life, not just while training for tennis.

Cross-training was also used extensively. They played soccer on a regular basis. Not only did it provide a fun team sport, but it was great for developing agility, endurance, and expanded vision. Badminton was another regular favorite, as it helped develop quickness, especially in the first step of moving up and back. It also developed a great smash and quick reflexes at the net. Running hills and hiking were also mixed in regularly. Not only did it help rejuvenate them by being in nature, but it strengthened their legs and developed the ability to focus. These would often be combined with a variety of concentration and awareness exercises. Often there were periods of silence during the hikes. The players were asked to use all of their senses to develop awareness of their surroundings. One exercise was to see five different objects, then hear five distinct sounds, then feel five unique sensations on their skin, then identify five different smells. Occasionally they would even taste a berry, leaf, or fruit that was known to be safe. This ability to focus completely on one sense at a time created a keen appreciation of connection with the world while developing the ability to shut out everything except the one area they were currently placing their attention on. This really paid off in big matches when it was important to tune out spectators, distractions, and the score and simply be in the moment while playing each point.

This emphasis on mindfulness was what truly attracted Sam to the academy. Ever since writing his article for Aunt Harriet he had tried to play in the present moment. Now he was not being ridiculed for it, he was actually being given not just the time to develop his awareness but provided with new tools as well. Yoga was a regular part of daily practice. Emphasis was on excellent breathing techniques to assist in relaxation. Bodily flexibility was certainly developed, but even more emphasis was placed on integrating the body, mind and spirit into a single concentrated purpose. They learned to increase the energy vibration in the body and use it to connect to a higher energy source. They developed their visualization skills to a level in which they could engage all of their senses to truly experience the future moments completely in their minds. Even when it was raining or injuries prevented them from physically practicing, they would practice in the mind and get nearly the same benefit, and without the risk of injury.

The coaches were always looking for the latest methods of increasing the mental strength of the players. They experimented with music and developed different playlists for the kids to listen to in order to elicit certain moods. Music was often piped to the courts during practice to make it more stimulating. Colors were also used to evoke certain emotions, and each child experimented to find the color of clothing that gave them the most power and confidence while playing. Watching video was another key component of the program. Video sessions of them playing were often used, not just for technique correction and match tactics discussions but also to help players recognize how powerful they were and create archives to return to when they inevitably went through periods of low confidence.

The academy also had a huge video library of inspiring movies. This was part of the weekend entertainment, but the movies were selected very purposefully. Scary movies and pure action thrillers were not allowed. Those chosen always had an inspirational story line that the kids could relate to and could stimulate great discussions afterward. One of their common favorites was Karate Kid and its sequels. Martial arts had not been part of the cross training at the academy due to its somewhat violent nature as well as potential for causing injuries. Tai chi and Qi Gong were used a bit for energy, but all other forms were not generally allowed.

One Sunday, after watching Karate Kid the night before, Sam was walking around the mall, not something he did often, but that day something compelled him to go. He followed his instinct and found himself standing in front of a kiosk that was promoting a non-violent, self-defense oriented form of martial arts, Aikido. He was drawn to the energy emanating from the booth, and especially one of the girls there. She was about his age, yet her eyes shone with a depth of joy that was startling. She radiated a power and confidence that was overwhelming, but she was extremely friendly when Sam asked her what her name was.

"My name is Lana, what is yours?"

When Sam replied, Lana said, "Hey, Sam. You look like an athlete. You wouldn't be from the tennis academy would you?"

Sam was stunned almost as much by her insight as he had been by her beautiful blue eyes. "How did you guess that?"

"I sense you have a strong motivation in your life, and the academy students I see here are always very polite and have a strong connection with their purpose in life. They are very different from most athletes I meet. They are much more like the kids I meet who are involved in Aikido. Do you do any martial arts training in the academy?"

"No." Sam replied, "They're too violent and can cause injuries that can hamper our tennis practice."

Lana moved closer to Sam and touched him on the shoulder. "Then you haven't tried Aikido," she said. "It's not about attacking or trying to hurt anyone. It is all about energy. The goal is to allow your energy to be so fluid that you can deflect any attacker by simply moving with their energy and avoiding contact or injury. Instead of trying to confront the energy of the opponent you simply dissipate it with your own energy. It's pretty amazing. Do you want to try it?"

"Sure," Sam replied, as intrigued by this girl Lana as he was by the concept of Aikido. "Why not? What do I do?"

"Simple. Just try to attack me."

"What, do you mean, like, try to hit you or grab you or kick you?" Sam asked, incredulous.

"Sure, try any and all of those. Don't be afraid and don't hesitate."

Sam sure didn't want to hurt a female, especially the fascinating one standing in front of him. So he made a slow, half-joking punch in her direction. The next thing he knew, he was on the ground looking up at Lana.

"Wait a minute. What happened?"

"Try again." Lana laughed. "You can do a lot better than that."

Sam next went with a kick like he had seen on Karate Kid. He had been practicing it a lot to improve his balance, and this time he put his entire focus into it. But the result was the same. He did a somersault through the air before landing on his back.

"Are you okay, Sam?" Lana said with a note of earnest concern in her voice. "I don't want to hurt you."

"No problem. I'm okay. I think I just lost my balance. Give me another chance. And this time you're the one who had better be careful. No more holding back."

"Okay. Give me your best effort."

This time Sam tried to grab her from behind after giving her his best head fake. Somehow he ended up with his arm locked behind his back and Lana totally controlling his ability to move.

"Give up?" Lana laughed gleefully.

"Never," Sam said.

He fought to break free of her hold but was totally unable to. He could tell she could really hurt his arm if she wanted to and was glad she was being gentle with him. No matter how hard he tried, it was impossible to break free. After a moment of struggle he realized how much he enjoyed being this close to a girl who had such incredible power and wielded it in such an easy and natural manner. He made a few more half-hearted efforts to escape, just to savor her touch on his body.

Finally he said, "Okay. You've got me. I give up. But you have to show me how you did that stuff."

"Giving up isn't that easy, Sam. I don't think you're a quitter, are you? So first you have to make me a promise before I release you."

"Okay, what do I need to promise?"

"Promise me that if you learn Aikido you will always use the energy for good purposes and will share it with others. Do you agree?"

"If that's what it will take for you to stop hurting me, okay I promise." Sam replied.

Lana immediately released him.

"Was I hurting you? I'm so sorry. I didn't mean to."

"No." Sam laughed while silently admiring her shoulder length brown hair. "You weren't hurting me. I'm tougher than that. I just wanted to make you feel bad."

They both burst into uncontrollable laughter. Sam felt lighter and more alive than he could remember. He had never encountered anyone who had this kind of magnetic energy. He knew he wanted to spend more time around this girl who seemed to exude unlimited joy.

The questions just burst out of him. He wanted to know where she was from, where she lived, how she had gotten into Aikido, where she went to school, who her friends were. The only question he hesitated to ask is whether or not she had a boyfriend. Although he desperately wanted to know, he didn't want to risk hearing the answer he feared. So he came up with an idea that would ensure he would see her again.

"Lana, do you think you could bring your Aikido master to the academy sometime? It would be great if he and you could teach some things to the rest of the players. We work on how to use our energy positively, but this is way beyond anything we do. What do you think?"

"I think it would be great. I can give you his phone number and your academy can call him to try to arrange a time."

That wasn't the direction Sam had in mind, so he had to think fast. "You know, both your master and my director must be very busy people. Why don't you talk to your master and I'll talk to mine? Then we can set up all the arrangements without them having to waste their time on it."

Lana replied, "I'm really not supposed to give out my phone number. My parents are pretty strict and old-fashioned that way. They always want to protect me. But after I got into Aikido they realized I can pretty well protect myself. I guess if they know it's to help spread the knowledge of Aikido they'll think it's okay. Here's my number. Please give me a call."

On hearing that, Sam's heart took a somersault. He figured she probably didn't have a boyfriend yet if her parents were that strict, and she had said PLEASE call me. That one word had given him a glimpse of hope that she might have some of the same feelings about him that he had about her.

"Sure," Sam replied, trying to sound cool and not overly anxious. "I'll try to call you, but we aren't allowed much phone time at the academy. Perhaps I can get special permission since we're working on this project together."

"Okay, do what you can. I look forward to hearing from you. Before you go, do you want to have one more try at taking me down?"

"Sure," Sam said, looking for any excuse to keep this magical connection alive. "Watch out this time."

He came at her with a punch that she dodged then a kick that she easily used to tip him over on his back with her on top of him, pinning him down. They both lay there and felt their hearts beating in unison and breathing heavily. They realized it wasn't from the exertion of the exercise, but rather the excitement of being that close together. After a glorious moment that Sam would cherish for a long time, they both jumped up in slight embarrassment.

"Well, my new friend, Sam. Guess you have a lot to learn. Hope you are faster on the tennis court than you are in fighting."

"Don't worry about that. Once you teach me a few moves perhaps I'll get over my hesitation about attacking a girl. I'll try to give you a call soon. I'm so glad I met you today."

"I am too. I look forward to your call."

As soon as Sam returned to the Academy he rushed to talk to Andy about Aikido. Although Andy was hesitant about any form of martial arts training he could sense Sam's excitement and didn't want to diffuse it, so he gave permission to arrange the meeting. Sam went straight to the phone to share the news with Lana. It was amazing how many phone calls back and forth it required to set up one simple meeting. It seemed like every detail had to be discussed at length, along with many other topics.

After a week of phone exchanges the day arrived. All the players were waiting to greet the Aikido master, but Sam was only interested in seeing Lana again. He dared not hug her as he would like, but instead politely shook her hand, trying to let his eyes convey what he was feeling for her. He knew the phone calls had solidified their friendship, and he was anxious to help it grow further. When her luminous blue eyes met his he instantly knew she felt the same way about him, and his heart skipped several beats in joy.

The Aikido master wasted no time. He immediately started talking to players about the similarities between Aikido and tennis. He said both are forms of one-on-one combat that are basically non-contact. They are both forms of energy exchange in which you are attempting to neutralize the power of your opponent while establishing the dominance of your own energy. The constant back and forth of the tennis ball is the same as the back and forth thrust of moves and energy in Aikido. To be successful a participant must always anticipate the moves of the opponent and train himself to instinctively reply to it in the most appropriate manner. This must be done not with muscle and conscious effort, but rather with a trust in your own energy to respond automatically. One who is too reliant on the strength of either the body or the mind will not be effective against an opponent who is well grounded in spirit and in full control of their energy. Instead of demonstrating Aikido, he asked for a volunteer to play him in tennis. Of course, everyone looked at Sam, since they knew it was his idea. Sam was ready for anything but this, but nevertheless got his racket and went out on the court. He could see that the guy had no training and no strokes, but he was able to block the ball back with just a little pushing motion.

After a few hits, the master said. "Okay, let's play."

Sam felt bad about picking on such a beginner so took it a little easy on his serve, which was easily returned. Sam started to move the master around the court, yet somehow he seemed to be standing waiting for the ball no matter where it was hit. Sam started hitting harder and harder, making the master move constantly for each shot, yet no matter what Sam tried the master was there to block the ball back. Thirty shots into the first point the guy was still getting every ball back. They were such easy returns that Sam decided not to hold back and started going for winners. He hit three straight shots close to the line that should have been outright winners, yet the master was miraculously in the right spot. Even his best attempts at disguising his shots had no impact on the master's uncanny ability to know exactly where he was hitting the ball. Sam was getting exhausted, frustrated, and embarrassed all at the same time. Finally on the fortieth ball he hit for the line with all his might into what appeared to be an open court. He wanted the point to finally end. It did end when his ball landed outside the singles sideline and the master was there to nonchalantly catch the ball in his left hand while calling it out. Then he gave a deep bow of respect to Sam. He was not even breathing deeply while Sam was sweating profusely and gasping for breath.

"Thank you for the nice demonstration, Sam." The master began as he tightened the black belt around his waist, "Sam has many skills and much training in tennis. He is an excellent player. I have no training and no skills in striking the ball. I have only one skill that is important in tennis. That is awareness. Yet my single skill enabled me to defend myself against the vast skills our friend Sam possesses. Just imagine how unbeatable Sam will be if I can teach him the skill of awareness to add to all of the other tools he has."

Sam slouched a bit more in embarrassment as he heard these words.

"Tennis is also about attacking and defending, just like Aikido." the master continued. "The Aikido master never initiates an attack; but he is always ready to defend. You see that if you can defend properly and expend little effort in doing so you can completely exhaust the strength of an aggressive attacker. It is simply a matter of accepting the energy they send to you and redirecting it in a way that blunts their attack. A great defender will always frustrate an attacker, and that must be your first priority."

On hearing this, Andy nodded in agreement, as it confirmed his philosophy that a solid defense must be the foundation of any successful tennis player.

Sensing Andy's approval the master resumed, "Of course, in tennis you have to be able to attack as well, but you should also do so with awareness and by using your energy effectively. Do not scatter your energy randomly or give up your power to your opponent by losing control of your emotions and succumbing to anger and frustration during the match. As soon as your opponent sees those emotions from you his energy grows and his confidence will increase exponentially."

Chapter Nine

After this demonstration of the importance of energy and focus, the players were very enthusiastic to learn Aikido. The master arranged to come twice a week to help them develop their awareness through a variety of exercises that never seemed to make any sense, yet after going through them the results were there and the purpose behind them was understood. Of course, Sam was overjoyed. Part of it was pride in the part he had played in bringing this new dimension of energy awareness to the academy. Part was the validation of the previous work he had done with his awareness techniques. The most important reason was that Lana joined the Master at almost every session as his assistant. Sam loved nothing more than to be in her radiant energy, and he lived for the times when he volunteered for a demonstration and was able to touch her when she would invariably throw him to the ground or pin him in a hold.

Gradually, as he improved his skills he was able to hold his own with her, and one day he was actually able to anticipate her moves and get the best of her. It seemed like his energy and hers just flowed back and forth naturally as if they already knew each other's mind. It was an amazing sense of unity. Sam was falling in love with Lana, a sensation he had never felt before. He longed to spend more time with her in private, but the Aikido sessions were the only times he saw her. He was not allowed personal phone calls, so the days of those early calls were over. Andy was very strict about allowing these kinds of affairs to interfere with the rigorous training that the students were undergoing.

Tina was especially sensitive about the time required for the players to handle their education. Although many academies throughout the world tended to downplay the importance of education and actually insist that their students quit school and devote all their energy to tennis, Tina and Andy were just the opposite. They recognized what a long shot it was for their students to make a living as a playing professional. In spite of their efforts to create the ideal environment for success, there were too many things that could derail a potential professional career. An injury or accident could happen at any time that could permanently limit future progress. Family and emotional issues often prevented necessary development. Many great talents found they couldn't handle the grind of constant travel and living on planes and in hotel rooms. Often the best junior players discovered they didn't have big enough weapons to win against bigger and stronger opponents, and many of them simply stopped growing and never reached the physical stature that has become more and more a necessity in the modern game.

Understanding these long odds of becoming a professional, then why did Andy and Tina devote their lives to helping students sacrifice so much of their childhood chasing such an elusive dream? They understood that the pursuit of a dream, even one that seems impossible, is what fuels all success in life. They knew that the skills their students were developing through tennis were giving them the tools necessary to achieve excellence in whatever career path they ended up choosing. Tennis forces young people to develop skills like time management, self-reliance, emotional stability, concentration, quick decision-making, positive reaction to failure, social skills, perseverance, self-belief and any number of other essential leadership skills. These real world success skills are seldom developed in a normal classroom setting the way they are in a safe and nurturing environment like a tennis court.

Andy felt these skills were much more important than any of the academic subjects taught in school that often have no real-world application. But Tina understood the value of the group setting of a classroom and also understood most parents' apprehension about their children cutting all ties with traditional education. Tina had exhaustively researched all aspects of education and had created what she felt was the ideal balance for the academy students. She had worked out an arrangement with a local school for players to be part of the school and get their testing and all diplomas through them. All academy players were required to attend two four-hour classroom sessions per week unless they were away at tournaments. The other days, players were required to spend at least three hours under Tina's supervision studying the course work from school as well as the online and other resources that Tina had put together. These were often not traditional subjects. She taught them speed reading and how to develop memory. She had courses in public speaking where they practiced handling media interviews successfully. They learned how to travel effectively and how to manage and invest money.

Geography was particularly emphasized so that they not only knew the map of the world, but learned about the history, culture, and language of locations. They even tied geography into the schedule of tournaments of the ATP, WTA and ITF. Each week one player would study and make a presentation to the others on the customs of a country in which a tournament was being played. A big aspect of culture was the religious customs of the countries, so all kids were exposed to the ideas of all of the major world religions and even some of the more obscure spiritual beliefs of indigenous cultures. By openly studying and trying to understand the essential premise of each system, the students gained a respect for the similarity of the foundational teachings of each one. They learned to appreciate the differences in the details of worship of each path while realizing that all were ultimately coming from the same source. When they made the connection that everyone on the planet was a small part of a larger power that had created the entire universe, then it made everyone the same. That understanding alone enabled the students to view all races, colors and nationalities as fellow souls and not as strange, foreign races. The students were becoming international ambassadors who would help bring goodwill and understanding to all the various cultures they experienced during their careers. They loved the opportunity to experience more of the world on the ITF junior circuit so they could begin to learn first-hand about the people and places they had studied in class. Because of the experiential nature of their academics at the academy the regular classrooms they attended tended to be dry and boring by comparison. Few of the students were excited about the time they had to spend in the classroom and did so grudgingly.

At the start of the new school year they were excited to learn that a different school had been selected for them to attend. It had a reputation of being much more open and progressive than the previous one. The difference was felt immediately on the first day of classes. It felt almost as comfortable, stimulating, and supportive as the academy did. Sam was really excited by the energy he felt in the school. His excitement increased a hundredfold when he caught a glimpse of Lana ducking into a classroom. He couldn't believe he was going to be able to see her two more days out of the week at her school. He made a note of the class she was in and made sure he was the first one to escape his classroom. He bolted down the hallway to reach her class before the rush to leave the room had begun. His heart was pounding, but he tried to look nonchalant when Lana finally emerged. No matter how much he tried to make it look like a mere coincidence that he happened to be going past her room when she came out, she could sense the truth.

"Wow, Lana." He stammered. "What a surprise to see you here. I didn't know you attended this school."

"O yeah, I thought you had researched everything about me." She teased. "I must admit, I was excited when I learned that your academy was going to switch to this school. You're going to love it here. It's an awesome school in so many ways."

"I'm sure that's true." Sam replied. "Right now there's only one really big reason why I'm glad we switched schools. Is there any chance of getting a personally guided tour from an experienced student who knows the place intimately?"

"Do you want me to find someone for you who fits that description?" She continued to tease as she smoothly slung her backpack over her shoulder.

"Actually, I kind of had in mind the student standing in front of me right now. Might she be willing and free at some time to do me the honor of a tour?"

"Well, I might be willing to take a Personal Discovery Hour right after lunch to show you around. Would that be okay?"

"Sounds great. What's a Personal Discovery Hour?" Sam said.

"Every week each student is allowed two Personal Discovery Hours. These can be taken at the student's discretion at any time with two exceptions. One is that it can't be used during the same class twice in a row. It also can't be used during an evaluation class. It's meant for a student to spend time alone in contemplation, often walking in the woods or in the meditation garden. It can also be used for envisioning a new project or finishing one you may have gotten behind on. Why don't you check and see whether or not you are allowed a PDH too, since you're only here for two half days.

Knowing your ability to charm people, perhaps you can swing a Personal Guided Tour Hour even if you aren't allowed a PDH. I'll meet you for lunch and see if it's possible. Okay?"

"Great. By the way, where's the cafeteria."

"No cafeteria. Lunch is served under that big veranda beside the meditation garden."

"Got it. See you there."

After the first morning, Sam was already blown away by the different attitude in this school. He could feel the energy and the friendliness of the students. It seemed like he had made more friends in several hours here than he had in an entire year at the old school. Although he knew that Lana was extra special, all of the students here seemed to share many of her wonderful qualities. They were almost all very open, curious, fun-loving and aware of the world around them as well as their own feelings and those of others. There was a sense of compassion and empathy for each other instead of the usual competition and petty jealousy that permeates most schools. By the time he met Lana for lunch he had a million questions about the school and how it developed those amazing qualities in the students.

Before he even had time to ask his first question after he had said "Hi" and had "accidentally" brushed his arm against hers (a habit he had developed to satisfy his need to touch her to remind himself that she was a real person and not just a figment of his imagination) he was struck by the lunch set-up. There were no lines with impersonal attendants mindlessly slopping industrial food onto a Styrofoam plate. Instead, the students simply sat anywhere they chose, most sitting on the wonderfully soft grass in the meditation garden. Fellow students did all the serving, from the plates and cups to the food. Each dish was personally brought around by the student who had just prepared it using produce from the organic garden. Each student was expected to take their turn in learning to cook. They took great pride in serving their creation and willingly shared what was in it and how they made it. It was very informal and seemed like the family style of a past era when families actually sat down together for a home-cooked meal. There were animated conversations going among each of the groups that formed on the lawn.

Lana explained that there were only two rules about the lunch process. One was that you ate all the food you accepted so nothing went to waste. The other was that no one ate alone, and you couldn't sit with the same person more than twice a week for lunch.

"Well, that's a relief," Sam said when he heard the last one. "Since I'm here only twice a week I'll be able to sit with you each time."

"How do you know I'll want that?" Lana said. "Or you either?"

Sam was stunned. He looked at her beautiful face and had no idea what to say.

"Sam, no matter how special our relationship is, I know you'll find many close friends here that you may like as well or better than me. Don't limit yourself in the number and kinds of relationships you have. You can have as many friendships as possible without taking anything away from those you feel are special. I'll never feel hurt or sad if you choose to eat lunch with others." As she spoke they both looked at the lawn and observed the numerous conversations being shared during lunch.

"I understand your feelings for me, but I don't want our friendship to limit your taking advantage of all of the opportunities this school presents. Let's finish quickly so we can have plenty of time for the tour."

Sam just gazed at her with his mouth full of a delicious dish of baked squash with zucchini and carrots. He was getting more enchanted with this girl every time she opened her mouth to talk. He was amazed at the wisdom and honesty that accompanied each of her words. It was so different than the gossip, nasty teasing, and competitive banter that had been prevalent at every other school he had ever attended.

He wanted so much to spend time with her, and he gave a silent prayer of thanks for the opportunity he had been given to be close to her at school. He loved every minute of the tour. There were so many interesting and unusual aspects of the school that seemed to make so much sense to him. He loved the fact that the entire place seemed to be completely integrated into nature. There was a gently flowing brook behind the school surrounded by a forest with numerous walking trails with benches available at regular intervals. Students were almost always seen walking in contemplation on the trails or sitting on benches in pairs or groups, talking animatedly yet softly. He was surprised he didn't see couples embracing or kissing like he had expected. In his heart that's what he wanted to do with

Lana, but he realized that these relationships seemed to be very respectful of the sanctity of the forest.

Chapter Ten

Just before entering the forest was the meditation garden that became one of Sam's favorite places to hang out. It was divided into separate sections for the major spiritual traditions in the world, yet they were all interlinked so it all seemed to flow together. The simple sayings from each tradition represented how similar they all are in their essence. The purpose of the garden was to help create respect for one's own tradition while at the same time understanding and honoring the beauty of all other cultures as well. It had an extremely calming energy. Students were encouraged to spend time there whenever they wanted to clear their minds and reconnect with what was most important in their lives. It was also the place where students were sent if there were any discipline problems. Instead of receiving a tongue lashing from the principal, students here were encouraged to reflect on their actions in a contemplative way and return with a renewed respect for themselves and for others.

The buildings themselves were all created in a circular fashion. This was to eliminate harsh lines and more closely match the forms of nature. It also made it possible for the entire class to sit in a circle. The teacher was part of the circle, and the center was for the person sharing. The curriculum was all about creating meaningful projects that were related to the subjects being studied and the issues facing the world in the present day. Students would discuss their projects and ask for ideas and assistance. Whoever was in the center of the circle was respected as the leader at that moment. Students developed excellent presentation and leadership skills and no one was allowed to hide at the back of the room. Everyone was always encouraged to share ideas and feedback, no matter how crazy it might seem.

Most of the projects were created by small groups working together, so much of the day was spent in small circles of students sharing ideas and creating strategies. Technology was used as an empowering tool for learning but was not a substitute for thought. Students had access to the internet, and if required, a large 3-D screen would be dropped from the ceiling into the center of the classrooms. This allowed the entire class to connect to watch videos, share online discussions with other classrooms throughout the world, and access virtually any knowledge available.

But the purpose was never to simply try to gain knowledge. It was always to develop the student's capacity to analyze, discuss, integrate, and use knowledge in order to create solutions to the problems of life. There were no exams and no high-pressure evaluations. Projects were given detailed feedback and were returned to be refined over and over until they were judged to be successful in the eyes of those who created them. Self-evaluation was done on a regular basis, with the students themselves assessing how well they had applied their focus and how much progress they had made. Even without exams and formal curricula, when the students took the government mandated tests or the SATs for college entrance, they almost always scored in the top 5% nationwide.

Many of the alumni of the school had gone on to become very successful entrepreneurs or had become famous in the fields of arts, sports, or design. Sam was very impressed with the tour of the school. Everything seemed so right to him. He felt truly blessed to have been led to both the academy and this school that seemed to be so aligned with what he had embraced through his mentorship with Aunt Harriet. He felt at home in a place where his talents and his spirit could soar to any height with no limitations. These were the happiest years of Sam's life. His tennis game continued to improve until he was ranked number one in the country in the 16s. He played enough ITF tournaments to be ranked in the top 10 in the world as a junior. He loved the idea of traveling internationally and actually experiencing the locations they had studied about at the academy. He was being touted as perhaps the next tennis great, and at the same time college coaches were actively trying to recruit him for their teams.

Meanwhile on the home front Sam had a number of very close and supportive friends. They helped prevent him from letting his ego get out of hand because of his success on the court. He was constantly surrounded with other kids who were successful in their own fields of endeavor, so they were neither jealous of his achievements nor hesitant to urge him to reach for even greater heights. Of course, Lana was always his closest friend, but it remained only that, a very dear and devoted friendship. They both focused on providing understanding and stability for each other when it was most needed without getting into the possessive attachment that typifies most teenage romances. Theirs was not a romantic relationship, just a nurturing friendship in which they both felt comfortable sharing their deepest and most secret feelings and fears.

Sam's greatest fear was how he would be able to cope with the reality of life on the tennis tour when he left his beloved academy and school. He had met enough of the pros when he played the junior grand slam tournaments to know that everything on tour was based on competition. The friendships were seldom deep, and were definitely forgotten when they faced each other across the net. He had met and heard about a number of junior phenoms who had lost their confidence while trying to make the transition to the pro game. For some it was the constant travel they couldn't handle. Others couldn't cope with losing first round regularly when they had been used to winning most of their matches. Others couldn't handle the different foods and constantly changing schedules that disrupted the pattern they had become accustomed to. Others just got lonely without the support of family or coaches, as few could afford a supportive entourage like the stars. Some fell victim to injuries due to the constant and extreme physical pounding the body had to endure in tennis. Others simply didn't have the weapons and the power to compete with older and more experienced players.

Sam didn't want to become just another example of a great junior who never made a mark on the pro circuit. He began to give serious thought to the idea of attending college. He knew this was a major decision in his life. The truly great players often made their presence on tour felt while still a teenager, like Raphael Nadal had. Some players had gone to college for a year or so like John McEnroe and then made it to the top. But most of those who went to college for more than one year seemed to have lost a couple key years, and although their careers may have been successful, they seldom seemed to have made it to the top. Sam tried to talk to as many pros and former pros as he could to get their perspective on this dilemma.

Although their answers all differed, there were many similar themes. Virtually all of them who had made it into the top twenty said they might have stunted their development by going to college. They felt the transition to the pro ranks had been relatively smooth. But in talking to those whose rankings never got beyond the top hundred he got a totally different story. Most said they wished they had gone to college for at least a year or more. They said how tough the first couple years were and how little support of any kind there was, emotionally, financially, and technically. The chance to go to college on a tennis scholarship and have all expenses paid while pursuing an education seemed to make a lot of sense to Sam. He loved the friendship and sense of teamwork he had with the others in the academy and he felt that being part of a college team would be similar. He didn't want to grind it out on the circuit for a couple years hoping he would have enough money to survive when the expenses for each tournament created a huge financial burden.

Finally, he turned to an advisor who had started a company specifically to help athletes in many sports from all over the world connect with the right university and the ideal scholarship program to meet their needs. Sam was very impressed with the company's professionalism. They helped him determine what college he would be most suited for. It didn't have to fit just from a tennis point of view, but academically and culturally as well. Sam had decided to major in business, although he knew tennis would be his career for as long as possible. Eventually he decided to attend one of the perennial tennis powerhouses located on the West Coast. One of the main reasons was that the coach had been a long-time friend of Andy's and he felt the same love of the game that Andy had. He was also known for developing players to become mentally tough and prepared for the pro circuit. He was tough in practice, but his love for his players shone through in the relationships he developed with them.

In the summer before starting college, Sam played a number of ITF futures and satellite tournaments both at home and overseas. This was a good opportunity to test his skills against professionals. The prize money was minimal, and he couldn't accept what he won and still be eligible for college. Fortunately, a friend of Andy's agreed to sponsor him so his expenses were covered. He was encouraged by his results, making it to two semi-finals and winning one doubles championship. He realized he was capable of competing against good players. But by the end of three months straight of tournament play he was very glad he was going to college. He couldn't see himself playing and traveling like that continuously throughout the long eleven-month season.

College started out very well for him. He loved the tennis practices, and the coach was able to recommend a variety of changes that really helped his game. He was focusing on developing the offensive weapons he would need to really make a mark on the pro level. His serve speed increased until he could reach 125 miles per hour. Even more important, the coach taught him how to serve intelligently. Instead of trying to hit a big ace on every first serve, he developed a driving topspin first serve that he could vary anywhere from 105 to 120 miles per hour and create subtle variations of spin and placement in addition to power. All of a sudden he found himself holding his serve easily, partly because his first serve percentage was so high that he constantly kept his opponent on the defensive. He didn't have to let up much on his second serve, and he still had the big bomb available at the key times in a match.

The coach also taught him how to look for offensive opportunities and take full advantage of them. They constantly practiced attacking a second serve with an aggressive forehand and following it into the net. They practiced volleys much more than Sam was used to at Andy's academy. This was partly to improve their doubles performance, but also to perfect their offensive skills. They were always encouraged to recognize when they had the opponent deep on defense and move in cautiously to hit a drive approach volley and follow it up with a winning volley. Sam loved that play, as it took advantage of his flair for deception and surprising his opponent.

As much as they worked on offense, they didn't neglect defense. The lob was encouraged when in ultimate defensive situations, and they drilled incessantly on what coach called the cross-court jab. That is the driving cross-court topspin that clears the net by a wide margin and lands deep in the court. This is the set-up shot for all others, hoping to force the opponent to hit short to provide an offensive opportunity. Sam could hit the cross-court jab hundreds of times without making an error. It frustrated his opponents so much they often got impatient and went for a winner down the line, giving Sam the chance to move them cross-court to the opposite side. In this way he made his opponents run twice as far as he did.

As much as he was stimulated by the tennis, Sam was disappointed with most other aspects of the university. His roommate was not an athlete. In fact, he smoked and drank and liked to bring girls to the room at night, something that wasn't allowed, but he tried to get away with it. He even had the nerve to ask Sam to stay out of the room until he had finished with the girl. Sam agreed the first two times, but after that he stood up for what he knew was right and told the roommate he would not leave, and that if he continued to bring girls to the room he would report him to the authorities. Of course, that created friction between the roommate and Sam, but Sam didn't really care. He knew what was right and he had no interest in being friends with someone who had no integrity.

The classes were a let down also. He had become used to the opportunity to ask questions and become engrossed in stimulating real-world projects. He had loved collaborating with friends to use their imagination and creativity to develop something really meaningful. Here, most of his classes were introductory lectures with over 200 students in the class. There was little opportunity for interaction and even less for asking questions. Sam couldn't see how any of this information would translate into something he could use in his life. He struggled to keep up with the constant tests and quizzes, something he had no real experience with in his other school. Plus, the constant travel to tournaments and matches made it difficult to catch up. Finally he realized that if he just learned the secret of taking true-or-false and multiple-choice tests he could get reasonable grades without studying very hard. He knew he wasn't learning much though.

The toughest part was that he had no real friends he could count on like he could Lana and many others from his previous school. He missed Lana, who had moved to France to study art and philosophy. They had tried to write to each other, but gradually their communication stopped as both were engrossed in their own worlds. Lana had tried to cheer Sam up and help him see the positives in his situation and encourage him to affect his environment instead of being brought down by it. It had helped, but since he had no time to meditate or spend in reflection in nature, he soon found his attitude becoming one of frustration and impatience. As the year progressed he became more and more isolated from everyone at school. Even his teammates were not really friends, since everyone was competing for playing time. He had managed to work his way up to number one by the end of the season, and that naturally turned the older players against this upstart freshman. They weren't overtly mean to him, but he realized he didn't fit into their established clique, going out drinking and celebrating together after the matches. It seemed like the fact that Sam didn't drink set him apart from all others in the school, as most of the social life revolved around drinking.

By the time the NCAA tournament rolled around, Sam had decided he was ready to move to the pro circuit full-time. The tournament was a dream for Sam. He helped his school win the team title. He finished as runner-up in singles and won the doubles championships. Finishing on a high like that confirmed in his mind that he was ready for the big time.

Chapter Eleven

What he wasn't ready for was the reality of how tough it was to break through on the circuit. He played the same futures and challenger tournaments as he had the year before. This time the pressure of needing to win to make money took its toll. He started focusing on the result instead of the process of playing with joy that he had learned to do in the juniors. The financial pressures were intense. Even if he won a $15,000 challenger, the amount he made was barely enough to cover his expenses. If he didn't win it was certain to cost him money just in travel and lodging expenses. Fortunately, his father had a couple friends who had agreed to sponsor him during his first year in exchange for a percentage of his prize money earnings once he made it big on the circuit. He began to get frustrated with his inability to win matches even at this low level. He got tired of traveling and playing every week in a different location. He had no friends, no coach, and no one to really motivate him to work on his game and continue to develop the skills he would need to play consistently well at that level.

After four months continuously on the circuit, Sam had to return home to beg for more money from his sponsors who were beginning to run out of patience. He assured them he was learning the ropes of the circuit and was on the verge of a big breakthrough. But when he visited Aunt Harriet she wouldn't listen to any of his rationalizations.

"Sam," she said, "I've been so proud of the way you handled yourself and the human being you became when you were at the academy. I was certain that not only could you create a good career for yourself, but that you would become an excellent role model for the upcoming generation. What happened to you in college that has taken you away from that joy you once felt from playing?"

"I don't know, Aunt Harriet. It just seemed like I had no friends to turn to for support, and I felt like I didn't have time for my meditation and visualization practices. Now that I've turned pro it's even worse. Not only do I not have any friends, but I don't have a coach, physical conditioning trainer or any support staff. I feel like I'm all on my own out there, and no one really even cares if I win or lose."

Ever the pragmatist, Aunt Harriet, simply asked, "So what are you going to do about it?"

Sam had gotten good over the past year or so at making excuses and placing blame. What he had lost was his ability to look deep within himself to find the answers.

"I don't know, Aunt Harriet. Maybe it's time to give up this crazy dream of pro tennis and go back to college to get my degree and go into business."

"Well, that's one option. But you couldn't go back on scholarship since you're now a professional. So how would you pay for school? It seems to me like you're sort of in a corner with your back against the wall. Are you going to give up so easily, or are you going to use this time at home to reconnect with who you really are and come up with some answers?"

"I guess you're right as usual, Aunt Harriet. I don't really have too many options, so I had better do everything I can to make this work. Before I leave I'll have some answers to share with you on what I'm going to change. Thanks for always being there when I need you."

Sam cancelled his entry in the next week's tournament so he had two full weeks at home. He spent most of the time walking on his favorite trails in the woods and meditating for hours in the solitude of nature. He could feel his connection with nature growing stronger. He was able to meditate for long periods of time. His breathing became deep and purposeful. He would sit for hours with a clear mind and simply focus on each breath coming in and going out. As he continued this process he eventually began to uncover the cause of his struggle. He realized he had removed his heart from his play. He had stopped playing with the joy that had always fueled his progress. Instead he had been focusing on the prize money and expenses and the entire process had been about money. He now realized that this mentality was constricting his skills and causing him to become anxious and tight in pressure situations.

Sam realized that in order to achieve his goals he would have to make the score the least important part of his thought process. He would need to focus on ensuring that he concentrated on giving his full effort on each and every ball. He would need to regain the joy of simply hitting the ball and trusting that his body would respond with the most effective shot for every situation. He began to see himself in his mind playing with the passion and joy that he had once taken for granted. He spent hours visualizing himself playing matches in which he was coming from behind to win the match, always with the focus on his performance, not the score. His movements in his mind seemed to flow naturally and spontaneously and he trusted that the result was always a positive one.

Sam's favorite meditation style was to immerse himself in the sound of the brook gurgling through the park. He allowed his mind to become absorbed in this sound until he could actually feel the water from the brook seemingly flow through his heart. In this state, everything seemed to slow down and he had a tremendous clarity in his ability to envision his life and his game. He could actually feel the shots and even hear the sound of the ball coming off the strings. In two instances, he seemed to move way beyond the tennis court and seemed to travel off the planet and begin to visit different dimensions in the universe. He was a little shocked by this, but the feeling he had was one of such peace and joy that he knew he had accessed something very special. He felt information being transferred to him in a form that was without words and that did not enter his mind. Rather it was felt as a knowing in his heart.

He purposely did not hit a tennis ball during this time. He wanted to allow the practice to take place in his mind so it could be pure in form and so he wouldn't have to deal with the frustration of making mistakes in real time. By the end of the second week he seemed to be completely at peace with himself and felt motivated to return to the tennis court. But not until he had paid a return visit to Aunt Harriet.

"Well, my dear Sam, what insights have you uncovered in the past two weeks?"

"Nothing earthshattering, Aunt Harriet. All I learned was that I have the strength inside to accomplish anything when I simply link up with the higher power and ask the universe for direction and help. My game is pure and ready if I simply trust in my ability and keep my mind from muddling the process of playing. I know I'm ready to return to the circuit and start to accomplish all that I'm capable of."

"Very good, Sam. You've learned the simplicity of what truth is. When you trust your inner guidance you're capable of achieving anything, as long as your focus is on the idea of giving your best effort without worrying about the score. You must trust that the results will come eventually if you simply unleash your connection to the highest power, the power that is within you."

How right Aunt Harriet was about results coming! At the first tournament, Sam won the championship in both singles and doubles. He followed that with a second successive satellite win and then a third in a row. All of a sudden his ranking began to climb as did his bank account. More important to Sam was that he was playing loose and relaxed tennis with a joy and freedom that he had barely remembered from his junior days. Tennis was fun again, and not just because he was winning. Rather he was winning because he was truly in love with this game that had always been his passion.

Suddenly he was the talk of the circuit and once again being touted as a star of the future. When he received a wild card into his first ATP tour event, a reporter wanted to know what had fueled his turnaround.

He decided to simply say, "I remembered how to trust the inner guidance that is coming through my heart."

This left the reporter dumbfounded. He had never heard a tennis pro talk in these terms before.

While he stammered to find a follow-up question to this most unexpected answer, Sam continued. "All the players have great skills, but most have self-doubts that they can actually achieve the highest levels. I know I've been blocking my true ability by thinking too much about the score, the money, ranking points, and so many other things. The more I think, the more doubts come into my mind and I begin holding back on hitting the shots I know I can hit. I took a couple weeks off, didn't touch a racket or hit a ball. I simply reconnected with my heart and my essential nature. I visualized playing with joy and being present in hitting every ball. This visualization is very powerful, and often it's better practice than actually hitting balls. I think young aspiring players should learn to visualize and use it consistently, spending about half as much time visualizing as they do on court hitting balls. I guarantee it will help the development of their game as much as it did mine."

At this point, Sam brought his thoughts back to his hotel room at Wimbledon. He had been so immersed in his visitation of his past that he had completely missed his scheduled time for yoga and stretching. He quickly called the physio to arrange another time. Then he realized that the physio was at his beck and call, since there were only two competitors left. That was something Sam had never experienced before. Even the hassle to book practice courts was a no-brainer. Then he realized the problem was getting a practice partner. Sam always had many players who were eager to hit with him since he was so focused and had such great energy during practice sessions. But by today they had all left the tournament. He certainly wasn't going to practice against his opponent in the final. Then he realized that the veterans event was still in progress. Maybe he could ask one of his former idols like Bjorn Borg or Pete Sampras to hit with him. As he researched, he realized that Andre Agassi was on the grounds. Did he dare ask Andre to hit with him? Why not? He was in the Wimbledon final. One thing he had learned from one of Aunt Harriet's favorite sayings was, "If you don't ask, you won't get anything. The worst that can happen is they say no, and then you are no worse off than if you never asked."

When he got Andre on the phone, Andre's praise of his game threw him off guard. Sam could feel the genuine admiration in Andre's voice as he accepted the invitation to practice in two hours. Then Andre asked if he wanted to meet an hour early just to talk. Sam eagerly accepted. Sam had many questions to ask Andre, as he wanted to learn all he could from this legend who had retired just before Sam made it onto the big circuit. But Andre beat him to the first question as he rubbed his famously bald head.

"Sam, why do think it took you this long to reach the finals of a major after so many years on the circuit? What enabled you to finally break through?"

"You know how difficult and lonely the circuit is," said Sam. "You benefitted greatly from having a strong support team that got you though the challenging phases of your career. Look at how fit and strong you still are due to the incredible physical conditioning you endured with Gil Reyes. I had fantastic support during my academy days; but during my career on the circuit I've been lacking that. I've struggled to consistently play with the clarity and conviction I know I'm capable of. My game is based on playing with joy and trust in my abilities and the higher powers. I simply hadn't been able to connect consistently with that trust to achieve high level results on a weekly basis."

The sun suddenly shone out from behind the clouds as Sam continued, "I haven't told anyone what has changed recently, but I feel comfortable sharing with you. My dearest friend during high school who brought so much joy to my life suddenly reconnected with me several months ago. She has given me the clarity of purpose to realize what I'm capable of. Every time I'm in touch with her I realize I'm capable of achieving anything. She's the only one who makes me feel like that."

"That's beautiful," Andre replied. "It seems like she has a similar effect on you as Steffi had for me. She helped me be very clear as to my purpose in life. When I'm certain that my life is meant to be in service to others, such as the kids at my school, then my play becomes infused with the idea of being successful in order to help more people improve their lives. Getting beyond my own selfish desires and fears was the greatest impetus to my success in the latter stages of my career. Where is this wonderful woman? I'd like to meet her."

"She isn't here." Sam replied. "I've only communicated with her on Skype and phone. I haven't seen her since I left for college."

"She's had that much impact on your life and you haven't even been with her personally? Wow. She must have some incredible energy. She will be there for the finals, won't she?"

"I don't think so. She's someplace in Africa where she's doing volunteer work."

Andre's face lit up as he flashed a sincere smile. "You must get her to the final. Phone her now and find out where she is. I'll send my private jet to pick her up and fly her here in time. I know how important it is to have someone this special be there for the final. There's no experience in the world that compares to playing in a Wimbledon final. You must ensure that everyone who loves you and has impacted your life profoundly is there to share that moment with you. Trust me, you'll always regret it if she isn't here with you."

Sam was blown away by Andre's generosity. "Do you really mean it? You would send your private jet to pick her up?"

"Yes, of course. My pilot is standing by now awaiting my instructions. I was planning to return home to Las Vegas this afternoon, but there's no way I would miss the final with you playing. You'll need all the support you can get to win this match, including mine. Now make the phone call quick so we can get our practice started and I can run your butt all over the court!"

Sam had never been more eager to make a phone call in his life, except possibly his first ever call to Lana to arrange the Aikido demonstration. When he finally contacted her in Nigeria she was so surprised and happy to hear his voice that she blurted out, "You were fantastic in the match. Good luck in the final. I know you'll do your very best."

Sam was overjoyed. "Lana, you know my sudden improvement over the past few months has been due to the inspiration I've gained by being back in communication with you. You've always been the person I've learned the most from and loved the most in my life. I want to dedicate this final to you. To do that you've got to be here in person. There will be a jet coming to pick you up at the Lagos airport this evening so you can arrive by tomorrow morning. Andre Agassi's pilot will contact you to arrange the details. And, by the way, what's your dress size? I need to buy you a dress that will match your beauty as we dance together at the champions' ball after I win the final."

"Sam, that's so beautiful. I don't know what to say. Thank you so much."

"Don't thank me. Thank Andre. Just be sure to get ready to meet the plane. There isn't much time left."

"There isn't much time left for you either. You'd better go practice to be ready for tomorrow. But before you go I want you to know one thing."

"What's that?" Sam replied, the sound of his heart in his ears.

"I love you, Sam. I've always loved you from the first day we met. I can't wait to see you again."

"I feel the same way about you, Lana. From the first time I looked into your beautiful blue eyes I knew we had the most incredible connection. You've always been the love of my life. Can't you just leave Africa for good and travel with me?"

"I don't know," Lana teased. "You may not be able to support me on the runner-up check, but if you have the $1.8 million champion's purse, perhaps I'll consider it."

They both laughed, unable to control their obvious love for each other. "Truthfully, I'm just finishing up my commitment here. I'm ready to follow you to the ends of the earth if you really want me to."

"I want that more than I want to hold that champion's trophy….. and check!" he said. "If winning is what it will take to have you with me full-time then that will be one more great incentive to win the match. Gotta go practice now, and you have some packing to do. I love you, Lana. I can't tell you how eager I am to see you tomorrow."

After Andre made a quick call to his pilot, he and Sam ran out to the practice court. They shared a magical hour running each other around the court with joyful enthusiasm that only comes from a deep love for the sport. At the end of the practice, Andre said, "Sam, I know you're ready for this match. Don't worry about anything. Just keep focusing on your joy and you'll have a fantastic experience in the final."

"Andre," Sam said as he bent down to pack his bag, "How can I ever thank you for this kindness?"

"There are two things you can do to thank me."

"Sure. What are they?" Sam said, somewhat surprised that Andre would actually place some conditions on the gift he had just bestowed.

"Number one, win this match. Our society only honors the champion, not the runner-up. There are lots of Wimbledon finalists who are forgotten, but a Wimbledon CHAMPION is never forgotten."

"Wow. I've never thought of it that way before," Sam said. "You're right, every Wimbledon winner is a household name, while many great finalists have been forgotten by all but tennis fanatics. Okay, what's the second condition?"

"The second is the most important. Use the fame you gain as Wimbledon Champion to create something that will provide a fulfilling life for you by enabling you to give back to the sport and create opportunities for kids to achieve their dreams like you have."

"That's beautiful. Do you mean I should establish a school for children like you did?"

"That was my dream, and its realization is what has fulfilled my life after my retirement," Andre said. "You'll find something equally worthwhile and satisfying that is your unique dream. Do you promise to do this for yourself, not for me?"

"You bet, Andre." Sam said excitedly. "You know I can't promise you I'll win the final, but I'll definitely promise you that I'll create something wonderful for children and share many of the gifts I've been given and things I've learned."

"That's all I can ask," Andre said. "But I also want you to win this match! You know you can do it. Now tell me what you'll do when you win match point."

"What do you mean?" asked Sam, shocked.

"You know every champion has their unique way of celebrating. Borg always went to his knees, Roger falls down on his back. I always bowed to all four sides of the stadium. I want you to visualize how you'll react when you finally realize your dream."

"Isn't that being a bit presumptuous? I always thought those reactions were completely spontaneous."

"Remember, the great champions visualize every aspect of the match so they're not surprised when the moment comes. Trust me, each of us visualized in advance exactly how we would react on championship point so we were never surprised or afraid of the moment when it came."

"That's amazing." Sam replied. "I certainly never thought like that before."

"Maybe that's why you've never had championship results until now," Andre said with a chuckle. "Now think about it and tell me what will be your signature response."

"Okay, but give me a moment to think," Sam said.

"Don't think about it. Just feel it in your heart."

"I see myself dropping to my knees and raising my arms to the heavens in thanks. Then putting my hands together in the prayer while bowing in thanks to all the supporters inside the stadium and throughout the cosmos that have assisted me in achieving this dream."

"Excellent. Now make sure this is a part of your visualization in preparation for your match. Pleasant dreams. I know you'll be ready for the match of your life tomorrow, Sam."

Sam could do nothing but simply bow and give a big hug in thanks to Andre for his wisdom, kindness, and friendship.

Chapter Twelve

A long shower and massage had never felt better than after this practice. But in the middle of the massage, Sam suddenly bolted up. He realized that he had failed to invite a few more key people to the final. So after making quick calls to Andy and Tina as well as Joe, and then requesting more tickets for the players box, Sam was able to settle down for the remainder of the massage with a clear mind and dozed off to sleep.

Suddenly he realized he had scheduled an 11 am news conference, and his Timex said it was already 11:11. He dressed hurriedly and walked out of the locker room into a sea of eager reporters, cameras, and microphones. The next hour was a blur of questions with Sam trying to answer as honestly as possible without giving them what they really wanted… some kind of scandal that would make the front pages. He was very careful not to mention anything about Lana, as he knew that was exactly what they were salivating for when they asked what had been his motivation to peak so suddenly after so many years with average results on tour. Instead, he talked about how important it was for him to play with mindfulness, clarity, and joy. He talked about the importance of meditation in his life and staying connected with the higher power. He knew this was too esoteric for them to try to sensationalize, and it got them to steer toward simpler questions like his strategy for the upcoming match. Finally the time was 12:12 and he reminded the reporters he had promised them one hour only. He felt empowered to stick to that promise and asked them to leave as he ducked back into the locker room. Fortunately, there was a back entrance that enabled him to escape to the car without facing the crowd again.

What he was not prepared for was the huge crowd of reporters and autograph seekers awaiting him at the entrance to his hotel. It took another forty-five minutes of signing autographs and answering questions before he finally made it to his hotel room. He was totally exhausted and was barely able to order room service, as there was no way he was going to face another hoard of admirers in the hotel restaurant. But he had one final errand on his mind. He called the jewelry store located in the hotel lobby. He asked if it might be possible for an employee to bring up some of their best diamond rings to his room in a couple hours. Then he finally fell into a deep and completely absorbing sleep.

As deep as his sleep was, it was not without lucid dreams that he had come to appreciate and remember throughout his life. But this dream was a very dark one filled with nightmarish situations he had experienced throughout his life. Every humiliation he had felt, beginning with his first time picking up a tennis racket, came back to haunt him. His humiliation at his first tennis academy sent waves of panic through his spine. He relived all of the times on the pro tour when he had looked foolish or lost matches by choking away huge leads. The dream ended with a nightmare of the final, where he tripped while bowing to the Duke and Duchess of Kent and made a complete fool of himself in the final, double-faulting twenty-three times and losing miserably. At the end of the match, instead of cheering for the winner the crowd actually booed Sam.

He awoke in a cold sweat. The dream made his entire life seem like a series of failures and made it seem that he hadn't deserved any of the success he had achieved. It brought up all of the doubts and feelings of lack of self-worth that he had experienced during his life. Although many of his dreams had come true, Sam recognized this dream not as one of seeing the future, but rather as one coming from the darkest part of his subconscious mind that was still trying to convince him he was a failure. It was the voice that had haunted him throughout his career, the lack of self-belief that had caused him to lose matches he should have won.

With one hour until his wakeup call, Sam knew he had to wipe the fears of the dream out of his mind. He first allowed all of the fears to come into his mind and acknowledge them. He admitted to himself that he was afraid of making a mockery of the final. After getting all his fears to the forefront, he focused on his heart and felt the love he had there. He felt his love for his family and all of his friends and supporters. Next he focused on his love for Lana. Finally he concentrated on the greatest gift she had given him recently, the ability to truly love himself. He felt himself filled with love and through that love felt connected with the totality of creation. He felt at one with the universe and at peace with himself. In that state of mind he bolted out of bed full of energy and quickly dressed just as the doorbell rang.

The jeweler had brought up an assortment of beautiful diamond engagement rings for Sam to consider. He lifted each one and felt the energy of it. One particular one seemed to attract him and he asked his inner knowing if it was the one for Lana. Then he visualized how she would react when he offered it to her and how it would look when he placed it on her finger. He was convinced it was the perfect one for her, and after negotiating the price down a bit, asked the jeweler if he could run his credit card in a couple days, after he received his Wimbledon check. When the jeweler realized this was the Sam he had been reading about in the newspapers he immediately offered to reduce the price by 25% and hold off on the credit card. Sam was surprised by this and began to realize that the way people treated him would certainly change, especially if he became a Wimbledon champion.

With the entire evening ahead of him, Sam knew he needed to be very thoughtful about how he spent this time, as he knew how important the night before a match is. If he went out to celebrate or mingle with fans, who knows what time he would return and what state of mind he would be in? Although he loved being with people, he also understood how important it was for him to remain in the right frame of mind to ensure that he was at his best in about twenty-four hours when he would hit the first ball of the ultimate match of his life. He decided to lie down again and visualize the entire match. He began with walking out of the locker room, reading the sign above the doorway with the quote from Rudyard Kipling's IF…"If you can meet with Triumph and Disaster and treat those two imposters just the same…" Just thinking about that quote made him wonder whether or not he could remain in control of his emotions no matter what transpired the following day.

He continued to visualize, seeing himself bowing to the aristocrats in the royal box and proceeding to the warm-up. He visualized the entire match with himself playing great and winning every point. He even saw himself winning match point and doing the celebration he had described to Andre. He allowed himself to feel the elation of having won tennis' highest prize. He also pictured in his mind the awards ceremony and even practiced his champion's speech, being sure to thank his family and friends, the ball persons, the All-England Club, and especially the British crowds for all their support throughout the tournament.

After finishing his 'triumph' visualization he decided to follow it with a 'disaster' visualization. He saw himself throwing up in the locker room out of nervousness, and tripping over his feet when bowing. He saw himself being so nervous and tight that he double-faulted away the first game while losing the first set quickly 6-1. He continued to see himself playing poorly, but saw himself starting to hang in there and get into the points. Finally he saw himself clawing his way back from a nearly impossible deficit to eventually pull out the match in five nail-biting sets. He knew the reality would likely lie somewhere between those two scenarios, but he wanted to be certain that he would have the strength to overcome the inevitable challenges that any closely contested tennis match produces. The thing he would not allow himself to visualize was losing match point or giving the runner-up speech. He knew that visualization must always leave you with a positive outcome and an optimistic mind set.

By the time he finished, it was after 7 pm, about the time he figured he would be holding one of the trophies in his arms the following day. He ordered room service for his favorite 'night before match' meal of gluten free pasta with vegetable filled tomato sauce, a Greek salad, and creamy dark chocolate mousse. After checking his email inbox and scrolling down the hundreds of congratulatory and good luck ones while responding to a couple essential ones, he settle down to watch a movie.

He was excited to find the movie "Greatest Game Ever Played" was available. It was one of his most inspirational movies, and he could certainly relate to its hero, Francis Ouimet, the hometown prodigy who overcame all odds (with the help of his ten-year-old caddy) to win a challenge match against the two greatest golfers of the era, Harry Vardon and Ted Ray. Watching the movie again was a fantastic way for Sam to fall asleep with the real-life inspiration of someone who had risen to the greatest heights at the biggest stage of his sport. Sam was just hoping he could do the same the next day.

Chapter Thirteen

As was typical before an important match, Sam slept fitfully, getting up almost every two hours to go to the loo, as they call it in England. He knew this meant he was nervous and would be ready on match day. He had learned a long time ago the importance of trying to get a regular amount of sleep each night, but not obsessing about it in the crazy world of professional tennis where you might finish one match after midnight and then have to play around noon the next day. One of the greatest challenges that prevented many excellent juniors from succeeding on the pro circuit was the incredible flexibility required to constantly adjust eating, sleeping, fitness workouts and practice to the scheduling of matches. You never knew from one day to the next when you would be playing your next match or whether you would instead be flying to the next event if you lost today's encounter. It was a challenging lifestyle and was certainly not suited to someone who had to rigidly follow a set schedule in order to be at their best.

When Sam finally awoke at 8 am, he remained in bed for another hour to do his final visualization, a combination of both the triumph and disaster versions that would hopefully be somewhat similar to the match, but of course with the desired outcome for Sam. While getting out of bed, he felt a sharp pain in his hip. What a horrible time for an old injury to suddenly flare up. He could barely limp around the room hoping that getting the blood flowing would cause it to go away.

No such luck. He wondered what could have caused it, then remembered a tough ball he had lunged for against Agassi. It had only registered slightly then, but now it seemed to have been a real recurrence of one of the injuries that had definitely slowed down his career. He quickly called Maria to see if she could come to his room to give him a massage. Knowing it was strictly against the rules for a tour therapist to visit a player's room, he called her supervisor to see if it would be okay in this situation. The supervisor said it would be allowed under these circumstances, but only because it was Sam and they knew it would not lead to any problems or potential scandals created by the British tabloids getting hold of something major. Because of this, they had to carefully plan how she could enter and leave the hotel without anyone, especially the press, knowing it. With millions of dollars being bet on the outcome of the finals, the hint of an undisclosed injury to a finalist could drastically affect the odds being placed on the match. Sam had never had to concern himself about these aspects of the game before, but now he understood the importance to the integrity of the game of many of the seemingly ridiculous rules.

It took Maria over two hours using all of her intuition and energetic skills in addition to her knowledge of Sam's body to help the hip become tolerable. Despite Maria's best attempts to be gentle the pain had been excruciating, and Sam felt it was more pain than he could possibly experience playing the match. He hoped the adrenaline flowing through his body would enable him to play through whatever pain he might face.

Now his timing had been delayed and he had to decide whether he had time for breakfast and lunch or opt for a larger brunch. The timing of a pre-match meal is always a challenge because of the uncertain starting time of a match. A final is one of the few times when players know their exact starting time and don't have to wait until the previous match on court finishes, which can be in as little as forty-five minutes or can stretch to over three hours. Knowing the final would start promptly at four o'clock let Sam plan more easily. He decided to have a small breakfast of oatmeal, strawberries and toast. As he was finishing breakfast he got a call from his Dad and Aunt Harriet from the airport. After explaining to them how to find the tournament transportation, he arranged for them to join him for lunch at 1 pm at the hotel.

Normally he would have gone to the tournament site for a solid warm-up a few hours prior to the match. With the status of his hip uncertain he decided he would forego that process and just rely on the ten-minute pre-match warm-up. He knew this was risky and could definitely backfire on him, but he couldn't risk having the hip take any unnecessary pounding. He decided to simply stay in the hotel room and concentrate on visualizing and doing some loosening up exercises to keep his body, especially his hip, as warm and supple as possible. He also did a number of little racket and ball control exercises that always helped him develop the feel for the ball. As lunchtime approached he was disappointed that he had not received the phone call he was most eager for, Lana announcing her arrival at Heathrow airport. He hadn't heard from her, Andre or his pilot since yesterday, so he could only hope all had gone well. His concern about her safety was forgotten when his Dad and Aunt Harriet arrived at his hotel room door.

"Dad, I can't tell you how much it means to me that you are here," Sam blurted through his tears.

"I'm so proud of you, Sam." His father said. "You've made me the happiest father in the whole world today. I can't believe I am actually going to be able to watch you play at Wimbledon Centre Court."

It was Aunt Harriet in her long brown overcoat and peacock-feathered hat that beamed with the most pride. Sam reached out and drew her into a teary-eyed hug.

"Aunt Harriet, you are the one who has made this moment possible. How can I begin to express how much you've meant to my life, and especially the way you kept Dad and me from hating each other because of tennis?"

"You already know the answer to that one, Sam dear." Aunt Harriet said. "Just go out on center court and show the entire world what a brilliant, courageous, and aware man you've become. Now, enough slobbering. Let's get something to eat. I'm starving, and you, young man, have to stay on schedule. Don't want to keep royalty waiting at center court."

Lunch was a time of wonderful reminiscence of the highs and lows they had experienced during Sam's childhood. They laughed when they all finally realized how skillfully Aunt Harriet had dealt with their crisis years ago. Sam felt closer to his Dad than at any time in his life and felt nothing but appreciation for the love he had shown. Suddenly they realized it was half-past two and Sam had to hustle to get prepared for the match. He still had not heard from Lana and this played on his mind as he rushed back to the room to pack his bag, something he had neglected to do earlier because of his preoccupation with his hip. He liked to get to the tournament site with plenty of time to spare, but now he realized he was late. The inevitable traffic for the final put even more pressure on the driver of the Rolls Royce, and Sam struggled to keep his mind calm during the ride. He kept checking his phone to see the time, but also in hopes that he would receive the eagerly awaited call or text from Lana. Instead he kept getting calls from the ticket office to confirm all the people who had suddenly been invited to the players box. Sam knew he had exceeded the normal allotment, and it took all his charisma to convince the girl in charge to honor all the requests and especially to hold one ticket for Lana, even if she arrived late.

By the time Sam arrived at the Wimbledon grounds it was 3:30. With the match time scheduled for 4:00 he was behind schedule to complete his normal pre-match ritual. The constant press wanting to ask him questions on his way to the locker room took additional time and energy. By the time he reached the sanctity of the locker room he barely had time to change into his tennis clothes and do a final check of the equipment in his bag. Although his usual routine was to visualize the match for thirty minutes just before going to the court, he realized that he had barely ten minutes to visualize now. Just as he closed his eyes Andre Agassi entered the locker room.

"How are you feeling, Sam? Are you ready to give it your all today?" Andre said.

"Truthfully, Andre, I'm feeling a little rushed and very nervous right now. I haven't heard from Lana yet. Do you know anything about her?" Sam asked.

"Everything's under control. She was picked up at the airport in Lagos and should be here any time. I haven't heard from the pilot yet, but he should call any time saying they've touched down. He'll make sure she gets to the stadium as soon as possible. Let me take care of that. You just need to focus on the job at hand. Be prepared for the biggest emotional rush of your life when you step onto the court and don't be surprised when your knees feel like they will buckle due to nerves. It's part of the process, and you'll get over it. I have a great feeling about your chances today. I know you're a champion human being. Now show the world you're a champion player also."

"Thanks so much, Andre." Sam said. "I feel a lot better now. Guess it's time to head to the court."

As Andre gave him a big hug Sam felt Andre's strength in his heart as well as his body. Sam hoped that some of Andre's championship qualities had rubbed off on him, because at this moment he felt nothing but nerves and fear. This was it. He was ready to walk out to finally try to fulfill his dream of winning Wimbledon. All he really felt like doing was throwing up.

Chapter Fourteen

If the London bookies had known about Sam's hip injury or even his state of mind trying to deal with the emotion of his family, friends, and Lana coming to see the match they would have made his odds of winning the longest in history. As it was, he was a five to one underdog against his opponent, a three time Wimbledon champion who had easily won his way through the field to enter his fifth Wimbledon final. The difference in experience was obvious as they took their first steps onto center court. While his opponent walked with supreme confidence bordering on cocky arrogance, Sam felt like a little kid who had snuck into the yard of a wealthy person's mansion. He didn't feel he belonged on this hallowed court. He would have walked right past the royal box if he hadn't practically run into his opponent bowing elegantly before the representatives of the royal family. Sam almost fell over as he gave a hurried, self-conscious bow.

The only thing that seemed to go right for Sam was winning the coin toss to determine choice of serve or side. Sam had such low self-confidence that he chose to receive first. This is practically unheard of at the professional level, especially on grass where the serve is such an important weapon. Sam simply didn't want to have to serve before he had a chance to clear some of the nerves out of his system. As they hit the first few warm-up balls, everything felt foreign to Sam. He was moving tentatively and still feeling a weakness in his hip. The pace of his opponent's shots caused the ball to miss-hit often and he felt no fluidity in his shots. Not having practiced earlier in the day to get a feel for the ball was hurting him now. Even his service motion in practice seemed stiff, and he didn't have the confidence to push up normally off his bad hip. He desperately wanted to warm up for an extra fifteen minutes or so, but the television schedule dictated that they begin right on time.

As he returned to his seat before the first game Sam looked up to the player's box. He was excited to see his Dad sitting next to Aunt Harriet, and he gave a little wave of recognition to Jay. The face he most wanted to see, Lana, was nowhere to be found. He found Andre who gave him a thumbs-up and a big grin. Sam forced a grin back at Andre, but in his heart he didn't feel happy. The experience was beginning to resemble the nightmare dream he had suffered through the other night. No matter how hard he tried he couldn't rid his mind of all of the doubts and negative thoughts that came flooding into it.

The first set was over in less than twenty-five minutes, and Sam was lucky to win one game and at least avoid the embarrassment of losing a love set. The second set didn't start any better, with Sam losing his first service game. Fortunately, he was gradually getting a feel for the ball and felt like he was at least warmed up and moving better. But playing a great player, he would have to be playing his absolute best. It seemed he had no chance of coming back. He hung on to win his serve the rest of the set, but still lost it 6-4, with the set taking only forty-five minutes. At this rate he would go down in the record books as losing the fastest men's final in Wimbledon history.

He decided to take a bathroom break at the end of the second set. He legitimately needed it, but probably would have taken it strategically anyway just to regroup and try to figure out how to make a comeback. He looked up to the sky, hoping to be saved by the inevitable Wimbledon rains that would give him a chance to recuperate. The uncharacteristically blue sky gave him no hope for a reprieve. As much as he tried to clear his head in the couple minutes in the locker room, all he could think of was how he was letting down all of the family and friends he had invited as well as the millions of TV viewers throughout the world who had been inspired by his underdog status and were hoping he could unseat the reigning champion. They had probably all given up hope by now, just as Sam had.

Arriving back on court, Sam sensed that something had changed. He felt an energizing breeze blow across the court, and he sensed immediately that his prayer had been answered. Looking to the player's box he saw the most beautiful sight of his life. Lana had finally arrived, and she glowed with the look of an angel. Although he had often tried to visualize what she had grown up to look like, he could never have dreamed that she could look this stunning. His heart skipped a beat as she nodded to him, and he gave her a genuine grin of absolute joy. He knew now that his inspiration had arrived. He was glad that tennis was such a forgiving sport. Even if you had been playing miserably there was always a chance that you could fight back and turn the match around. No match is ever over until match point is won. It takes tremendous courage to finish a match, and the great players learn to never give up and to persevere to the end, no matter what challenges they may face in the match.

Sam decided that the best way to turn the match around would be the surprise tactic of serving and volleying. Although this had been the most effective style of play on grass for years, in the last decade the serve and volley had become nearly extinct, as the service return had seemingly taken control of the game. Sam had always enjoyed playing serve and volley, although he used it only as a way of keeping his opponents off balance. This time the surprise worked and he quickly won the first three points of his service game. He was inspired by Lana's presence and knew that he was now right back in the match. At forty-love he served an excellent kick serve out wide and came in behind it. The opponent miss-hit the ball so badly that it flew in the opposite direction he had planned. As Sam tried to change direction his hip suddenly burst into a searing pain that brought him to the grass at the service line where he lay watching helplessly as the miss-hit ball landed softly a foot inside the sideline. He lay there for nearly a minute, afraid to even try to put any weight on the hip. To his surprise, despite the pain he was able to stand up and gingerly walk around. The trainer had already come out to the court and helped him return to the sidelines. By the time he arrived there Sam seemed to be able to move more easily and it appeared to be just a temporary pain caused by the sudden movement. Of course, no one except the trainer had any idea what he had gone through with the hip earlier in the day.

Sam didn't want to lose the momentum he had created, so when he realized he could walk without a limp he signaled that he could continue to play without taking a full injury time out. As he started his serve at forty-fifteen he felt a sharp pain when he tried to explode up off his left leg. His first serve landed meekly in the net.

Fortunately, one of the exercises he had used extensively as a kid was serving from one knee to get the feeling of hitting up and using the wrist to create power. On his second serve he was still able to generate a relatively solid topspin serve. It wasn't enough to put pressure on a top player, and his opponent promptly hit a service return winner. On the next point Sam went for a big first serve without using his legs. It was in, but the return was deep to the backhand corner which Sam barely reached and floated back, giving his opponent an easy put-away at the net. Deuce. "So much for momentum," Sam thought.

He did his best to put pressure on his serves, but without the extra fifteen percent power generated from the legs it was impossible to put his opponent on the defensive. Instead, Sam found himself scrambling after returns and struggling to return them. He lost the next two points to go down a break in the third and most likely final set.

At the changeover Sam seriously considered retiring. He had a built-in excuse with the hip injury, and he didn't see any way he could play at the level needed to win with limited mobility and not enough power on his serve. Just before going up to the umpire to announce his decision he looked up at Lana. She gave him a stunning smile and he realized she had only seen him play one game. How could he give up when she hadn't even seen him play the way he was capable of?

He assumed his ready position on the baseline with renewed determination. He would give everything he had to turn this match around, even if it meant being injured for the next six months. This was his chance to transform his career, and he wasn't going to go out without giving everything he had. The next four points were the hardest-fought points of the match. Both players were hitting hard to the corners and forcing the opponent to come up with impossible shots. At thirty-all Sam attacked a short ball and hit a knifing backhand approach shot deep down-the-line to the opponent's forehand. Sam knew the cross-court passing shot was his rival's favorite shot, so he played closer to the middle of the court to cover it. Instead his opponent nailed the shot down the line. The only chance Sam had to reach the ball was to launch himself in a complete dive. He slid the racket down to the last two fingers to maximize the reach. At full stretch he barely touched the ball, yet had enough control to get under the ball just enough to hit a perfect drop volley that landed two feet on the other side of the net and died in almost the same spot. A winner!

Unfortunately, Sam landed directly on the sore hip. He heard a cracking sound and felt the most intense pain of his life. As he lay on the ground he realized he couldn't get up without help and waited until the trainer arrived. When the trainer touched the spot and sent Sam into yelps of pain, it was clear to both that there was no way to continue the match. Before making the final decision, Sam looked again up to the player's box and his gaze met Lana's. Her look of concern for his well-being was matched by a calmness and confidence he hadn't expected. How could she be so cool when the person she supposedly loved was in such a terrible situation? Then with a slight smile she touched her temple while shaking her head. Then she touched her heart and opened her hands to him as if offering him the fullness of her love.

In an instant Sam recognized what she was saying. What Lana had taught him over Skype during the past four months was how to quiet his mind and instead engage his heart. It enabled him to connect with universal intelligence, the source of all energy, including physical healing. It was this technique that had enabled him to easily enter the zone state and play with the confidence that overcame all the self-doubts and limitations created by the mind. He also remembered a technique they had discussed called quantum healing in which amazing healing could take place simply by touching two places on the body and entering for a short moment into that gap between thoughts. With absolutely nothing to lose, Sam decided to try it. He touched the hip with his left hand and placed his right hand just above his solar plexus. With a final look up at Lana to assure himself that she was sending him her loving energy he quieted his mind and entered a state of pure awareness. The crowd no longer existed, nor did the court, the opponent, or even Lana. For a moment he was in another dimension feeling nothing but pure energy. He felt his hands practically burning and felt a searing heat enter his hip. He didn't even think about the injury, but only felt a sense of extreme gratitude surge through his body. He was simply in joy about being alive and having the opportunity to be engaged in living his passion and being surrounded by people who inspired him and were inspired by him.

In that state he had no awareness of time, and was surprised that less than one minute had passed when he returned to normal consciousness. The trainer was shocked when Sam announced that he was able to continue playing and rose to his feet on his own power. His opponent had already come to the net to see if Sam was okay, fully anticipating that this would be the end of the match. It wasn't the ideal way for the match to end, especially since the fans had not really seen much of a match, but he would have been happy to hold the champion's trophy no matter how he got it. He was even more startled than the trainer and the fans to see Sam declare that he was fit and ready to resume play. The trainer felt his hip another time and couldn't believe there was now no swelling and seemingly no pain. He had no explanation for what had just happened, but he was willing to take credit for helping Sam make a miraculous recovery from a serious injury. He had no choice but to give Sam the okay to continue.

Chapter Fifteen

In the TV operations van the director was trying to make sense of the drama happening on the court. His instincts told him something unusual was taking place between Sam and the mysterious girl in the players box.

"Who's the girl! Who's the girl!" he screamed.

"I need a name. Get me the name, Maggie" he yelled at the Cyron operator who was in charge of the on-screen graphics. "You have thirty seconds to get the name up on the screen."

"Courier. Get to the players box and get an interview with her….. now!"

"This match has been a sleeper so far, but we may have a Lazarus story on our hands. We gotta be ready for it. Archives, keep the semi-final cued up. He may still have to default or the chump may get blown out in the third. We gotta be ready for anything."

"Boss" said Jim Courier, "I'm on top of it. Already at the players box, but no one seems to know her. Not his dad or his aunt. All I got from his old coach, Jay, was that he thinks she must be an angel."

"Oh that's just great, an angel in the players box," ranted the director. "Courier, did you ask her? I want an interview with her."

"I tried, boss" said Jim. "She just waved me away when I tried to approach her."

"You really have a way with women, Courier. Don't try, just get me the interview. Now!"

"I have a name. It's Lana," said a visibly relieved Maggie as she got it ready to put on the screen.

"Glad someone can get something done. What's the story? Who is she?"

"According to Lisa at the ticket office she just flew in from Africa or some place. All she knew is that Sam insisted she hold a ticket for Lana, no matter how late she arrived."

"Sounds like a long-lost girlfriend. Courier, get me that interview. We may have some drama on our hands after all, gang. Let's get ready to ride this for all it's worth."

As the director was frantically trying to capture the drama on camera it was unfolding on court. Having reached break point with his lunging drop volley, Sam had ripped the first serve cross-court for a winner to get back the service break and even the set at one game all. On his service game he had served and volleyed twice for winners while winning the game at love. His opponent was trying to recover from having thought the match was over to now having to deal with a transformed competitor who was playing inspired tennis.

It took all his skill and experience to barely hold his service games while Sam easily held his serve. Sam was playing like a man possessed. Between every point he closed his eyes for a few seconds and then prepared for the next point with a look of total concentration in his eyes that signaled the perfect balance of intensity and relaxation. Sam was in the zone! The third set tiebreak wasn't even close, as Sam seemed to know where the serve was coming every time and hit two return winners to capture the set 7-2 in the tiebreak.

The capacity crowd was enthralled by the sudden turn of events and was cheering wildly for Sam. Wimbledon fans always cheer for the underdog, especially when one player is getting blown out and the fans are eager to see more tennis. But they were also sensing how special this level of tennis was and how inspired Sam had become. Their energy carried Sam to even greater heights of play, as he won the fourth set 6-4 getting the only service break in the seventh game. It was now two sets all with everything coming down to the fifth and final set.

Jim Courier had been going crazy, trying desperately to get an interview with Lana. No matter how persistent he was, she either ignored him or waved him away with a smile, never breaking her concentration on the energy that she seemed to be sending Sam. The camera couldn't stop focusing on Lana and panned to her after almost every point, yet her expression seldom varied from the look of calm beauty that was completely focused on her connection with

Sam. Sam's opponent was now getting desperate, sensing that his title was about to be taken away by a foe who seemed to be so completely in the zone that he could hit the most audacious shots without fear of missing. In fact, there had been so few unforced errors in the last two sets that almost every point had been won with a clean winner after long and unbelievably powerful yet varied rallies. He knew he had to do something to bring Sam back to reality or he had no chance to win the match. He approached the umpire at the changeover.

"George, you gotta do something about the illegal coaching that's going on. He's obviously getting signals from someone up there." He pleaded with the umpire.

"Come on," said the umpire. "It's just a girl. He doesn't even have a coach. I know something crazy is going on, but I can't call it illegal coaching."

Since that tactic didn't work, on the changeover he tried to break Sam's concentration by taunting him. "What's the matter, chump. Do you need to get signals from a girl in your players box to try to hang in the match?"

Sam recognized the mind game he was playing and was encouraged by this sign of desperation from his opponent. "Yeah. Don't you wish you had an angel in your box to inspire you?"

The fifth set began with the entire crowd being engrossed in the match. Each point was played at the highest level of intensity and positive shot-making. Winners were the norm, yet what should have been winners somehow were returned, with most rallies continuing for another seven or eight shots until a clean winner was finally hit. Each game was extremely hard fought, while each player continued to hold serve throughout the set. Was it possible for this high level of tennis to continue indefinitely until it was potentially stopped due to darkness, since there would be no tiebreak in the deciding set?

Sam continued his ritual of closing his eyes after every point and starting every point as if playing in a trance. He showed no traces of the hip injury and was moving around the court at incredible speeds. Neither player seemed to be affected by the fatigue you would anticipate after more than four hours of competition at this elevated level. If anything they seemed more energized and the shots became even harder, more varied and more precise as the match went on. Although the crowd was clearly rooting for Sam, they were wildly applauding the brilliance of every winner, and they recognized this was a magical match that neither player deserved to lose.

It was now seven games all in the deciding set with no seeming advantage to either player. Sam had played beautifully to reach thirty-all on his opponent's serve. As he took a deep breath and went into his trancelike state, his mind told him this was it. He finally had a golden opportunity to break and serve for the championship. Sam took another deep breath and allowed that thought to move harmlessly through. He knew if he dwelt on that thought, it put him into future thinking and would take him out of his state of flow. Instead, he felt his heart and drew another deep breath while focusing only on the target for his return of serve.

His opponent hit a slice serve that pulled Sam to the doubles sideline. Sam was planning to return cross-court and the wide serve gave him a tremendous angle. He hit a vicious topspin forehand that landed five feet inside the service line and forced his adversary to return it from four feet outside the singles sideline, where he realized he would have a tough time recovering, so he gambled and went for a winning forehand down-the-line. Although it was a low percentage shot, he had been successful making that shot all day, and he hit another beautiful shot. Sam was anticipating it and streaked across the court, but the shot was so good that Sam could barely reach it by stretching out completely with only one hand on his backhand. Most players are lucky to float the ball back from this position. Fortunately, Sam had often practiced using his wrist to get outside the ball almost like a squash shot. It was one of the fun games he had loved, seeing if he could return crosscourt even when the ball was way behind him.

Sam's shot was more than a floater. It was a sharply hit underspin that zipped cross-court over the lowest part of the net and landed two inches inside the side T, the intersection of the singles sideline and the service line. His foe could only look in wonder at yet another miracle shot that Sam had created off what should have been a winner. Now he was facing a break point that could give Sam the opportunity to serve for the championship.

The first serve at thirty-forty was a bullet hit at 137 miles per hour, aimed straight at Sam's belly. Although not often an ace, the body serve is often very effective at producing a weak return, especially when hit as a surprise with a lot of power. Although Sam was surprised by the serve, his instincts and his natural hop to get on his toes allowed him move aside enough to hit a solid return deep cross-court, preventing the opponent from gaining the offensive. Both players knew this was the most crucial point of the match so far and were totally focused. They continued a deep cross-court rally to the backhands, trying to force the other to hit short enough to give an offensive opportunity. After a dozen cross-courts with varying arcs and power, Sam took advantage of a slightly shorter ball to rip a backhand down-the-line. He knew it was a great shot that would put his opponent on the defensive, so he took three steps inside the baseline to be ready to take the offense. His opponent realized that if he floated the ball back Sam would have an easy drive volley into an open court. So he gambled again and hit a vicious cross-court topspin forehand passing shot. Sam wasn't fooled and was perfectly balanced before the opponent hit, so he was able to quickly lunge to his right and although stretched completely was able to guide a half-volley down the line deep to the backhand corner. His opponent was no longer surprised by Sam reaching even his best shots, so he raced to the corner and pulled the trigger on yet another passing shot down-the-line. Sam knew this was his only potential target and was in great position. Although he had to stretch completely again to reach the rapidly dipping ball, he got the lower edge of his racket under the ball and guided a delicately angled drop volley cross-court that died on the grass a foot from the opposite sideline. His adversary made a valiant effort to reach it, but even a dive at full stretch wasn't enough to get there before the second bounce. Sam had the service break and would now serve for the Wimbledon Championship!

Chapter Sixteen

One of the greatest mental challenges in all of sport is for the underdog in tennis to serve out the match to get a breakthrough win. Being that close to ultimate success usually brings up all sorts of old fears and feelings of unworthiness. Many players have completely choked in this situation, double-faulting meekly even if they had been serving brilliantly throughout the match. The mind can play such tricks and create limitations on a player's ability. On the other extreme are the greatest champions, such as Pete Sampras, Roger Federer, and Rod Laver who always seemed to come up with their best serves under the most pressure. Laver, the only man to have ever won two calendar year grand slams (winning the Australian, French, Wimbledon, and US Open in the same year) was so confident, his teammates would get out of their seats and head to the bar if Laver was serving for the match at 5-4.

"Laver always closes out the match when he serves for it, so we have to beat him to the brews," was their comment when asked how they could leave at a crucial juncture of a match.

In this crowd, no one was even thinking about leaving for the pub, as they realized that a historic match was unfolding before their eyes. As much as they wanted Sam to win, they realized what a challenge he faced and knew it was an even bet that the set would continue for at least another few games, if not as long as the epic Isner-Mahut match that ended at 71-69 in the fifth set!

At the changeover, instead of burying his head in the towel to shut out distractions and focus on the upcoming game, Sam's eyes went to the players box. He saw all the people who had meant so much to him over the years. He felt the love they had for him and the pride they had in his accomplishments. He felt his heart beating audibly, less from the tension of the match than the pure love he felt at that moment, not just from his box but from the entire crowd. He sought out Lana's gaze. For a brief moment their eyes locked. She sent loving energy directly into his heart while giving a slight grin and a nod showing her absolute confidence in his ability to finally achieve his dream. He put his entire focus on his heart. Instead of allowing his mind to entertain any limiting thoughts he simply felt how blessed he was to be in this position. He was poised to achieve the pinnacle of success that would give him a platform from which to have a tremendous impact on future generations.

Sam took one last glance up to Andre Agassi before closing his eyes to visualize the next game. He knew the best way to overcome nerves was to play aggressively and dictate the point from the beginning. He decided to serve and volley on every point. He was going to win it his way, by taking charge of the action. He played four perfect points in his mind, visualizing not only where he would serve but also where he would hit his first volley and then the second, if and when his opponent reached the first one. He finished his visualization by seeing himself winning match point and then going through the victory celebration exactly as he had described it to Andre just over twenty-four hours earlier. Since he had served and volleyed very selectively throughout the match he figured the surprise factor would put his opponent off balance. Who would expect such bold aggressiveness from someone who should be fighting with nerves in what should be the most tension-filled moment of his life?

Instead of tension, Sam felt excitement and joy. He knew in his heart that all the work he had dedicated his entire life to had prepared him for this moment, this opportunity to achieve his dream. He was not going to let his mind talk him out of the success he knew he deserved. Instead of walking deliberately to the baseline, he decided to run out, much like Rafael Nadal had always done, showing not only how strong and fit he was but also how excited he was to be playing this wonderful sport. His opponent took this as a sign of either nerves or foolishness and was fully expecting Sam to crumble under the pressure. He looked at Sam with a big grin, as if to say "We both know you were lucky to get to this point, but I know what it takes to win championships and you don't. Feel your legs wobbling, your heart pounding, and your arm tightening up along with your throat. Don't choke now…."

Imagine his shock when Sam's first delivery was a 120 mile an hour slice serve wide to his forehand that shot quickly off the grass. He was barely able to get his racket on it and guide the return down-the-line, only to get his second shock that Sam was at the net to knife away the cross-court backhand volley, just as he had visualized it. Fifteen-love.

"Okay, I give you credit for having guts, but there's no way you'll try that play again," the opponent thought. So he was fooled again when Sam rifled a serve into the center T at 132 miles per hour. Again, the forehand return was just a floater hit to a waiting Sam at the net. The opponent guessed right that Sam would try to finish the forehand volley cross-court and even though Sam hit it perfectly it was not a winner this time. His foe barely reached it and sent up a lob high into the gathering darkness of clouds and dusk. "That will give you time to think about the situation and tighten up," thought his opponent as he launched his epic lob into the sky.

The crowd held its collective breath as Sam elected to let the ball bounce, knowing how difficult it was to time an overhead coming straight down, especially with the swirling wind that had picked up during the past half-hour. The danger of letting a lob drop on grass, especially grass worn down by two weeks of non-stop pounding, is the possibility of a bad bounce. A gasp went up from the crowd when the ball hit a bad patch of grass and instead of bouncing straight up for an easy overhead, instead shot sideways and low. Sam had stayed on his toes and alert. He was able to lunge after the errantly bouncing ball and with a flick of the wrist guide it down-the-line to the backhand corner. His opponent had been delighted to see the lucky bounce and now scrambled to return Sam's shot. This time his weak return gave Sam a high forehand volley that he attacked with his feet, avoiding the tendency to get greedy and overswing, zipping a sharp cross-court volley for a clean winner. Thirty-love. Only two points from victory.

Now it was Sam's opponent's turn to feel the nerves. Throughout the match he had expected that Sam would choke at crunch time. He was surprised that Sam had been able to sustain his stratospheric level of play, but had assumed Sam would fold in the clutch as he had at various times during his career. Now he was realizing that Sam was playing bold, inspired tennis and was showing no sign of nerves. Nothing he had tried had been able to get Sam out of his zone. He decided to try one more strategy to play on Sam's mind. On the return of serve he moved four steps to the left of his normal returning position. His goal was to tempt Sam to repeat the wide slice serve he had used on the first point. He would be anticipating it and the plan was to pounce on it to hit a forehand winner down the line. He knew it would take a bold play like this to take the momentum away from Sam and his audaciously daring tactics.

Even though he saw the deliberate change in position by his opponent, Sam decided to stick to his pre-planned visualization play of serving down the middle and following it with a first volley also deep down the middle. The idea was to eliminate angles for passing shots and hopefully get an easy finishing volley on the third or fourth shot. Caught off balance as he moved toward the sideline, Sam's opponent had to change direction and lunge to reach the 125 mile an hour serve and was lucky to hit it solidly and quite low to Sam's forehand volley. Anticipating a drop volley from that position with the ball below net level, he moved in a step and a half. When Sam volleyed sharply and deep back down the middle he was again caught off-balance with the ball at his feet. All he could do was block back a lob that barely made it to the service line. Sam was there to calmly angle the overhead away for a winner. Forty-love. Three championship points for Sam.

The crowd was delirious as they all rose to their feet as one, cheering madly. They didn't want to see this incredible display of tennis end, but they were eager to help Sam complete this most improbable journey in a courageous if not completely audacious finish. Just one more point. Yet any tennis player knows that match point can be the largest hurdle to overcome, and a match is never over until match point is won. It doesn't matter how close you come if you cannot capture the final point. That is one of the things that makes the tennis scoring system so fascinating and such a wonderful lesson for life. You can never simply cruise across the finish line or protect a lead until the time runs out. The final point must be won, and there is always the opportunity to make a comeback no matter how far behind you are.

Sam was determined not to let the thought of match point enter his mind as he prepared to serve from the ad court. Somewhere in the back of his mind flashed his childhood dream of winning the final point at Wimbledon with an ace as the perfect way to end a match. With a cushion of three match points he decided to go for the ace up the middle, even though his original visualization was to serve and volley behind a kick serve out wide. After visualizing his target and taking a deep breath, he nailed a 132 mile per hour serve toward the center T. The crowd roared as the ball kicked up the chalk on the service line. Sam was sure he had hit it perfectly then saw the center service linesperson signaling it out while lunging out of the way of the speeding ball. Sam immediately asked for it to be reviewed as he glared at the linesperson who had robbed him of his dream ace. Silence engulfed the stadium during the fifteen second wait to see the result of the replay. The crowd went berserk, as did Sam when the huge screen at the corner of the stadium showed the serve missing the center service line by half an inch. So close to a dream finish, yet it was just a fault.

Sam couldn't believe it and tried to gather himself for the second serve. He felt himself getting angry at the linesperson, the replay system and also himself for abandoning his original plan. He hadn't visualized a second serve, and certainly didn't want to lose a match point by hitting a double fault. He rushed into his second serve without completely clearing his mind from emotion. The result was a tentative second serve that sat up easily for his opponent who fearlessly crushed a cross-court backhand winner that Sam couldn't even react to. One match point saved. Forty-fifteen.

Once an opportunity to finish the match has been lost, especially when it is so agonizingly close, the entire psychology of the two players often changes. Suddenly Sam started to feel the pressure of closing out the match while his opponent gained confidence by his perception of Sam finally showing signs of nerves. The fans were delirious, wondering if one more momentum swing was possible in this highly emotional match. Sam was so eager to put the memory of the last point out of his mind that he rushed to the line to serve on the deuce court. He decided to serve out wide to the forehand to open the court for a winning volley. His first serve was a wicked slice that missed the sideline by an obvious three inches. No replay needed for this one. He was faced with another second serve. Determined not to allow his foe another easy ball to attack Sam took his time and nailed a strong topspin serve up the middle… that dipped down two inches beyond the service line. Double fault. Second match point saved. One championship point remaining at forty-thirty.

Now Sam was really angry at himself. Was he finally choking after playing so brilliantly throughout the last three sets? Up in the TV booth the commentators began to sense a meltdown from Sam.

"What do you think is going through Sam's mind now?" John McEnroe asked. "Do you think he's finally going to crack under the weight of the pressure to win Wimbledon? I know this is perhaps the most difficult emotional position any tennis player can face, and Sam certainly hasn't been here before. I'm surprised he hasn't cracked before this, but match point is a completely different experience than any previous point. Let's see how he handles it, but his opponent is certainly starting to show more confidence."

Sam slowly circled ten feet behind the baseline to gather his thoughts as the stadium erupted with cheers and shouts of encouragement. The applause was a spontaneous expression of thanks to both players for the courage and skill they had displayed throughout the nearly five hours of perhaps the most entertaining tennis ever witnessed. Sam was overwhelmed with emotion as he felt the outpouring from the crowd. His mind was racing wildly between gratitude for the support and fear of losing another match point and perhaps the match. Before starting his service ritual he glanced up to his box one more time. Lana was a picture of calm in the bedlam around her. She gently placed her hand over her heart and smiled.

Immediately, Sam's mind cleared. He understood that not only was Lana saying that she loved him with all her heart but was also suggesting that he play this point from his heart and get his mind out of the way. His heart was pounding with his feelings for her as well as his nerves. He took a deep belly breath while closing his eyes. He decided to revert to his original plan on the ad side to serve and volley with a kick serve out wide and open up the court for a winning volley. He strode to the line confidently. He was back in the zone.

Instead of going for the ace he chose to hit a strong, safe topspin serve and rely on his volley to finish the point. He wasn't going to let his ego get in the way by gambling for a spectacular serve. He would challenge his opponent to beat him with a better shot but was not going to give away another match point with a double fault. Another deep breath relaxed him as he focused only on the intended target for his serve.

He exploded up into the serve, hitting a wide kick serve at only 108 miles per hour, taking a little speed off to ensure not only that the first serve was in but to give him time to approach the net. His opponent wasn't fooled and stepped into the doubles alley, unleashing a blistering topspin backhand that would have landed directly on the line. It was a perfect shot, a clean winner. Except that it never hit the line. Sam reacted instinctively, diving through the air at full stretch. He reached the ball and with the slightest flick of the wrist directed a sharply angled cross-court volley. His opponent never had the chance to react, as he assumed he had hit a winning return. Sam lay sprawled completely outstretched on the ground, hoping that his ball had been in. There was a moment of stunned silence. Then the crowd erupted, realizing that Sam's desperation volley had landed in for a clean winner. Match point, Sam. He was the Wimbledon Champion!

Chapter Seventeen

As he lay on the cool grass waves of emotion flowed through Sam's body. He was transported back to his earliest childhood memories laying in the meadow and watching the clouds blow past. He felt like his entire life had been leading to this moment and he was overwhelmed with utter joy. The bliss he felt in that moment was indescribable. He felt enveloped in a cocoon of love, feeling the energy of the stadium flow through him and transport him into a realm of pure happiness. Tears of joy filled his eyes and flowed down his cheeks. He also felt a huge sense of relief at finally overcoming all the demons in his mind and committing completely to achieving ultimate success. He had no idea how long he had lain there and he suddenly realized he needed to rise up and go through the ritual he had described to Andre. As he attempted to stand he felt something else, pain, shooting through his leg. In his all-out dive he had twisted somehow and reinjured the hip.

He was now aware of his opponent as well as the trainer standing over him, concerned at how long he had been still. His opponent offered his hand, as a sincere gesture of congratulations as well as an assist to help him get on his feet. When he tried to put weight on the hip it buckled in pain and the trainer had to support him also. He placed his arms on their shoulders and they practically dragged him back to the player's bench. Sam was still in a daze but was aware that every person in the stadium was standing and had been cheering and applauding ever since the last ball was hit. The noise was deafening, yet it hit another crescendo when he stood up and was able to limp along with assistance. Never in its storied history had Wimbledon witnessed the drama that had just taken place, and the fans were showing their appreciation in any way they could.

As the officials and staff bustled about in their efficient routine to prepare for the final trophy presentation of the fortnight, Jim Courier, mike in hand, approached Sam as he sat in his chair. Jim opened his mouth but no words came out. He simply shook Sam's hand and then bent down and gave him a hug.

When he could finally find words, Jim said, "I have a million questions I'd love to ask you, Sam. I have some idea of the emotions you're experiencing and would love for you to share them with all of us. But there's only one question my director and everyone watching wants me to ask......who is the radiant woman whose appearance in your box seemed to inspire you to play the incredible tennis that earned you the championship?"

Sam had no idea how to deal with the depth of his emotions nor did he know how to share Lana with the world in such a public way. He simply opened his mouth and the words that came out tried to make a joke. "You're right about her being the source of my inspiration, Jim. If she hadn't arrived you would all be at the pub right now talking about the most boring final ever and how painful it was to pay so much money to watch the journeyman being helplessly slaughtered."

There was a chuckle and knowing nods from most fans as they thought back to their feelings three hours earlier when it had looked like Sam would be dismissed in three quick sets. Sam's vulnerability made him seem more human and endeared him even more to the fans. Another spontaneous burst of applause filled the stadium and continued for another two minutes. No one wanted this beautiful flood of emotion to end. As the applause continued Sam looked up to his box and was again overcome with tears as he felt the love from all those who had meant so much to him. He asked Jim for the mike and continued.

"I had always visualized climbing up to the players box to hug my friends and family, like Pat Cash first did in 1987. But it looks like I'm in no shape to do that now. I know it's against protocol, but I would certainly appreciate it if my family and friends in the players box could be allowed onto the court to be with me during the awards ceremony."

The tournament director came up to Sam and said, "You know your request is highly irregular, but in this particular situation we will allow it."

While Sam's family was being escorted down to the court, the prize ceremony started with the introduction of the losing finalist. Although it was a crushing defeat for Sam's opponent, he handled himself very gracefully.

"I played the best match of my life and got beaten fairly by an inspired player who competed at a level unheard of in tennis. I thought I had the match well in hand until an angel entered Sam's box and give him some kind of divine energy. How can I compete with that? It was an amazing match to be a part of, and I want to thank all of you for spurring us both to shot-making brilliance that will be talked about for a long time."

After speaking he walked over to again assist Sam in approaching the podium, as Sam was still unable to walk under his own power. He gave Sam a big, sincere hug before handing the mike over to him.

As Sam was handed the champions trophy and held it over his head in triumph, tears of joy again flowed down his cheeks. Flashbulbs were popping all over the stadium to capture this most unlikely moment in Wimbledon history. The fans were again showering him with thunderous applause. Twice Sam tried to dry his eyes and prepare to speak, but the applause would not die down, nor could he find the words to begin. Finally, he motioned for his dad to join him on the podium. They embraced in pure love as the crowd continued to be engrossed in the extraordinary moment. Finally Sam was able to speak.

"You may not know it, but this is the first match my father has seen me play in-person since I was eleven years old. He loved me so much that seeing me pursue my dream was more important to him than his desire to see me play. Dad, I love you so much. Thank you for everything you've meant to me. I'm so glad you were here with me today. I could never have done it without you."

After similarly hugging and thanking his Mom as well as Jay, the coach that inspired his love of the game, he invited Aunt Harriet to join him. Although he still struggled to stand on his own, he gave her such a powerful hug that it knocked her hat off. The depth of the embrace was felt by everyone in the crowd, and although they didn't know who this person was, they sensed how important she had been in Sam's life.

"This woman, my Aunt Harriet, has been the guiding light in my life ever since I can remember. She has made me the human being I am today. If it weren't for her I would have given up the sport long ago or would have become the most obnoxious player in the history of the game. She has taught me more about life and about myself than anyone else. Aunt Harriet, thank you so much for being such a wonderful mentor, teacher, and inspiration to me."

After another hug, the crowd's attention turned to Lana, who was still standing in the middle of the court, the mystery angel that everyone was wondering about. Sam wanted to pique their curiosity for a while longer, while savoring every minute of the feeling of unity he felt with his family and everyone else in the stands.

"I now want to thank All England club and its officials," Sam began. "I want to thank the ball persons and all the volunteers who make this tournament so special for the players. A special thanks to my therapist, Maria, without whose help I would not have been able to get out of bed this morning. I want to thank the press for being so supportive and not prying too deeply into my private life." The last comment drew a chuckle from most in the crowd, as they knew how eager the tabloids had been to find something risqué to write about Sam.

"I want to congratulate my opponent for a fantastic tournament and for playing such a phenomenal match today. He is truly a champion, and I will always feel fortunate to have been able to join him in raising our games to the heights you saw today. Please show him again how much you appreciate his play today."

As the applause finally died down Sam continued "There is another champion in the crowd who I must thank. Andre Agassi is one of the most wonderful human beings ever to grace our sport. Without his encouragement and advice I could never have survived the pressure of today's match. You saw how nervous I was at the beginning, and without his advice I could never have made it past the third set. Plus, without his jet my inspiration would never have arrived in time to save me. Thank you from the bottom of my heart, Andre."

Another round of cheering went up for Andre, then a chant softly arose through the applause. "Angel. Angel. Angel. Angel." It began to increase in volume until the entire stadium was in unison.

"I know you feel I'm saving the best for last, and I am." Sam said. "Thank you all here in the stadium and watching on TV for the incredible support you've given me throughout my career and especially during this magical fortnight. Your love and energy has meant so much to me. Thank you. Thank you."

Again, the crowd went wild. Another full minute of wild cheering went by before the chant started again, "Angel. Angel. Angel. Angel."

Sam looked at Lana as the chant steadily rose in volume. Their gaze met and tears immediately started to flow again. Sam had looked forward to reuniting with Lana for over ten years and had never dreamed it would be in such a public setting. Finally, he motioned for her to join him on the podium. First their teary eyes met then their bodies embraced in a hug so powerful that it sent the crowd into another level of frenzy with their chant. The moment stretched into minutes as the love that had developed since the day of their first meeting flowed throughout their bodies. They were united at the heart in the most beautiful, pure energy.

Reluctantly, Sam let go of Lana and tried to clear his voice to speak. The first try didn't work. Neither did the second. The crowd began to laugh, sensing Sam's complete sense of overwhelm with all the emotions. Finally words came out of Sam's mouth.

"Ever since Coach Jay planted the seed of the dream of becoming Wimbledon champion, I've always thought it would be the happiest moment of my life. Now that I've experienced the moment, I can say it truly is my happiest ever. Yet even that moment has just been surpassed by the incredible joy of finally being reunited with my soul mate, my childhood sweetheart, and yes, my angel, Lana."

When the angel was finally given a name, the fans went crazy again, this time chanting, "Lana. Lana. Lana. Lana" Knowing he couldn't even attempt to speak over this tumult Sam simply embraced Lana again and held her tight while the chant continued to build in volume. It finally started to die down as the crowd sensed that Sam had more to say.

"We haven't seen each other in ten years, and it was only four months ago that we started to communicate again by Skype. Yet both of us have known since the first day we met that we were meant for each other. Reuniting with Lana is what has sparked my recent resurgence as a tennis player, and ignited my spirit as a human being. You all saw how her presence transformed me today from a chump to a champion. She is truly my angel, the love of my life. Lana, thank you for all you've meant to me over the years. We've shared a special kind of love that knows no boundaries of time and space. You've been in my heart every moment since the day we met."

Sam had to stop and wipe his tears with a handkerchief he pulled out of his pocket. Hidden in the handkerchief was a small box. He dropped to his knees, opened the box and said. "Lana, I want you to be with me physically as well as in my heart for the rest of my life. Will you marry me?"

Lana's sparkling smile and gentle nod said more than words could have, as the crowd unleashed a roar that would have drowned out any words. Sam placed the ring on her finger and they embraced again. It was a hug coming from love they both knew as the fulfillment of their dream that would last a lifetime.

About the Author

Ted Murray has been pursuing his dream of raising people's consciousness through tennis for the past 4 decades. A late starter to the game, he played Division 1 college tennis while during the summers learning to teach at a summer tennis camp. This grew into a 20 year career as a founding member of Peter Burwash International, an outgrowth of a dream to take the fun and joy of tennis to people throughout the world. Running tennis programs in 6 countries while traveling to over 30 with the PBI Tennis Show truly was Ted's dream. After moving on from PBI he has owned his own club in Florida, started tennis academies in 3 countries and has coached juniors who became Olympic medalists and multiple Grand Slam champions.

His dream has always included sharing his joy of tennis with others. He has spoken at numerous coaches conventions and co-authored the instruction book, Tennis Unlimited. He was deeply involved in Cardio Tennis becoming a phenomenon of fun and fitness worldwide, and is currently helping to launch a new tennis organization, the Tennis Legacy Fund, to help increase environmental awareness in tennis.

His major focus is his company, Tennis From the Heart. Its goal is to provide inspiration and tools to players, parents and coaches to make the experience of tennis one of joy, personal development and success in all aspects of life. He has been on a personal development quest while sharing messages from the heart with people around the world.

67016381R00076

Made in the USA
Columbia, SC
22 July 2019